JAMES HAMILTON-PATERSON was educated at Oxford,
where he won the Newdigate Prize. In addition to
journalism for *The Sunday Times*, *The Times Literary
Supplement* and the *New Statesman*, he has published
poetry and one previous collection of short stories, *The
View from Mount Dog*. The non-fiction work, *Playing with
Water*, was followed by his first novel, *Gerontius*, which
won a Whitbread Prize in 1989, and *The Bell-Boy*. In 1992
he published *Seven-Tenths: the Sea and its Thresholds*, a
blend of literature and science exploring the seas. His
novel *Griefwork*, published in 1993, was much acclaimed,
and his most recent novel, *Ghosts of Manila*, was shortlisted
for the Whitbread Fiction Prize in 1994. He lives in Italy
and the Philippines.

The Music

JAMES HAMILTON-PATERSON

Stories

JONATHAN CAPE
LONDON

First published 1995

1 3 5 7 9 10 8 6 4 2

© James Hamilton-Paterson 1995

James Hamilton-Paterson has asserted his right
under the Copyright, Designs and Patents Act, 1988
to be identified as the author of this work

First published in the United Kingdom in 1995 by
Jonathan Cape
Random House, 20 Vauxhall Bridge Road, London SW1V 2SA

Random House Australia (Pty) Limited
20 Alfred Street, Milsons Point, Sydney,
New South Wales 2061, Australia

Random House New Zealand Limited
18 Poland Road, Glenfield
Auckland 10, New Zealand

Random House South Africa (Pty) Limited
PO Box 337, Bergvlei, 2012 South Africa

Random House UK Ltd Reg. No. 954009

A CIP catalogue record for this book
is available from the British Library

Papers used by Random House UK Ltd are natural,
recyclable products made from wood grown in sustainable forests.
The manufacturing processes conform to the environmental
regulations of the country of origin

ISBN 0–224–04195–9

Typeset by Deltatype Ltd, Ellesmere Port, Cheshire
Printed and bound in Great Britain by
Mackays of Chatham plc, Chatham, Kent

CONTENTS

Acknowledgments

An earlier form of 'Frank's Fate' appeared in *London Magazine*, February/March 1990; 'Anxieties of Desire' appeared in *Obsession*, published by Serpent's Tail, 1995; 'The Last Picnic' was commissioned by the BBC, broadcast and published (in *BBC Music Magazine*) in 1994.

The quotations from *British Medical Journal* in 'Farts and Longing' are taken from *BMJ* vol. 305 (19–26 December 1992).

'I've never been to me' words and music by Ken Hirsh and Ronald Miller © 1975, Stone Diamond Music Corp, USA. Reproduced by permission of Jobete Music (UK) Ltd, London WC2H 0EA.

The Music (1)

ONE OF THOSE sharp moments which feels like a jab of sanity: standing at the supermarket checkout and suddenly being overwhelmed with fear. Something to do with the grey coat of the man up ahead, with the way he's gazing down into his wire trolley, with the numb bustle, the Saturday throng, the *throughput* of it all. The torrent of shoppers, the torrent of money, the torrent of goods, most of which last will have turned within days into a torrent of shit; then back again next Saturday to repeat the process. The sheer emptiness of having to maintain ourselves. Hunter-gatherers at a vacant shuffle. The grey-haired man in his neatly brushed coat. Why can't we all just agree to die now? Lie down and let the centuries roll us back into the turf.

From loudspeakers set invisibly among the acoustic tiles of the ceiling's white cloudbase falls The Music. The spongy sound is adhesive; we want to make peeling gestures like tearing off a pair of unbearably hot rubber gloves. But it affects no locatable part of the body and the urge persists as an itch unsatisfied. Anxiety levels escalate as though from a fear of choking. Possibly The Music neutralises oxygen. In any case it's closely associated with the supermarket smell which permeates clothing like ether or nicotine. Yet there is something not entirely man-made about either the smell or The Music. Hard to believe a man in a van could account for it all by delivering fragrance cylinders and tapes once a week. Maybe there's a clue in the way The Music keeps interrupting itself with random messages about special offers and staff calls to Till 9. It's a reminder that all forms of public address, from the bullying to the fatuous, tap an atavistic response. A supermarket loudspeaker announcing that a car is blocking one of the car-park exits is, however vestigially, the Voice of God speaking from a cloud. The foam-rubber music oozing down behind it is the sound the world turns to, the true Music of the Spheres. These voices come to us from above, from overhead, utterly null yet with associations of authority. In this celestial cantata the litany of car registration numbers is set to The Music's elastic waves, the one designed to grab your attention, the other to suppress it.

Everything of interest is elsewhere; we are here. Suddenly it's no longer foam rubber leaking from the ceiling but sand. The entire supermarket is a gigantic egg-timer and our time is racing through the holes in the acoustic tiles overhead and filling up the aisles with dunes which slow our feet to a weary trudge. Still we follow the sheeplike progress of the grey man ahead, pushing our wire trolleys meekly as between cemetery gates or through fireproof doors straight into a crematorium's blazing heart.

By the time we've reached the checkout we're knee-deep in death, and panic is building. That moment of sanity, the clear vision, has jolted us through the roof. Looking down, we see in ourselves an unknown species queuing for its life, its ears stuffed with foam-rubber music. Not so zombified that we don't notice a sudden gap at the next till, though; so when at last our trolley noses out into fresh air and sunlight and the foam rubber falls from our ears, there's the elderly man in the mohair coat just reaching his car. People are standing around it in stylised attitudes of ruffle and tetch which they can only have learned by watching television. *This* is how you stand, *this* the right expression of ill-concealed truculence when somebody's car blocks yours. For it is this charming, dignified, sane old creature whom the Voice from the Clouds had been addressing every few minutes: this his car, that its number.

'Stupid bugger!'

'Don't you care about anybody else, then?'

'I hope they've sent for the police.'

These are adults speaking, not their children. It's the absence of The Music that does it. Once we're out into the fresh air with our wire trolleys and The Music stops we're hit by the raw ache of wastage, by the whiff of crematorium smoke, by a panic to retrieve some of that sand and stuff it back into the timer. We don't know that's what it is, of course. What it is, is some daft old git blocking the exit with his potboiler car.

How wrong we were to patronise the back of his tall grey coat at the checkout! He elects not to notice these people, carefully puts his packages on to the rear seat, slowly opens the driver's door with a faraway glance at the air above the supermarket. It quivers with the heating system's thermals so a line of bare trees beyond dances in fake summer. The sunlight reveals he has two hearing aids.

'Deaf twit!'

'Shouldn't be on the road!'

He drives away, dignity personified. He was immune after all. He never heard The Music. He leaves those he momentarily discommoded furiously telling each other over and over again things they already know.

The Last Picnic

I SUPPOSE IT SEEMS strange now – contrived, even obsessive – that after our mother died my father used to take us children each year for a picnic on the same spot. He wasn't a religious man but maybe this ritual had about as much of the sacramental as he would allow himself, commemorating our last family holiday together.

From a summery backdrop one year suddenly emerged a small man in stained trousers and, despite the heat, a Fair Isle sweater with many holes among its jigsaw patterns. Sitting around our tablecloth spread on the ground, glasses of ginger beer balanced between tufts, we resentfully watched his approach.

'I am Dr Schumann,' this gentleman announced, looking at us in turn. 'I'm so happy you've found my favourite spot.' He extended his hand.

My father, half rising, took it courteously on our behalf, caught in mid-role between the paterfamilias put out by the intrusion and the experienced GP who smells derangement and opts for prudence. 'And I am Dr

Sanders. Yes indeed, a lovely spot. Er . . . we'll have finished with it by-and-by.'

'Ah, a medical man? I'm afraid I'm only a musician. You may perhaps have heard of me. Schumann? Robert Schumann?'

My sister Caroline and I saw an expression cross our father's face. It was the look when, in the middle of Christmas lunch, the phone rang and called him away to a bedside: noble, martyred, apologetic, and perhaps with the tiniest fraction of relief.

'You can't be *the* Schumann, the composer.' Caroline was the family's pianist. 'He's dead, you know. Yonks ago.' Maybe she caught the fierce glance our father shot at her but at thirteen, my elder by a couple of years, she was not so easily squashed. 'Why did you make everything you wrote so difficult, then?'

Our visitor looked very tenderly at her and said: 'You remind me of my darling Clara.' I could sense my father stir uneasily. 'She was a wonderful pianist, better than I ever became. I wrote nearly everything for her. What, in particular, are you thinking of?'

'Well, how about *Carnaval*? That's awful. I'm supposed to learn some of it this holiday.'

'But that's the very subject of a story I have to tell you,' cried the self-styled composer, leaning forward and plucking up our last sausage-roll with a squirrel's agility. 'Listen. You have to imagine I'm nineteen and already embarked on a career as a concert pianist. I was even

6

celebrated enough to have demonstrated Harrods'
Steinway collection. I played there an hour each tea-time
for a week in between engagements. On the last day a lady
approached me and said: "Maestro, this weekend we're
having a masked ball. You're going to play Schumann for
us, I've quite decided. You may name your own fee, but in
return you must agree to obey my instructions to the
letter. I'm determined you shall come. Dear, divine,
maestrino that you are – handsome, cheeky thing in
private, though, I daresay." She squeezed my hand. "You
shall dress as Schumann, of course. And – Clara awaits
you. *Such* a Clara, too. Dangerously young. Tomorrow
you will receive your instructions."

'What could I say? I was myself young, excitable, easily
beguiled by mystery. Promptly the next morning a
messenger arrived with a sealed envelope and a box
containing my costume. "Prepare yourself to play
Carnaval," the letter said, "even though we already know
you play it beautifully. Dress at five; drink nothing; the
carriage will call for you at six." I did as instructed. All day
I practised music which I'd long known by heart until I
could have played all twenty pieces in my sleep and – '

'I bet you had a hard time with "Sphinxes" ', interrupted
Caroline in that slightly-too-casual voice of hers which
generally meant a trick question.

Our uninvited guest was not in the least discomfited.
' "Sphinxes", of course, is not written to be played. It's
more symbolic: anagrams of the German musical notes

7

A, S, C, H. Asch is the name of a town in Germany where Ernestine, another little friend of mine, lives. The piece can be heard *in the heart, my dearest,* and you'll never play *Carnaval* well until you can hear my "Sphinxes" in your heart . . . So anyway, at five I dressed and waited with a strange excitement. At six the doorbell rang and I was ushered into the back seat of a tall Rolls-Royce whose windows were thickly curtained. A man in black handed me a blindfold which he respectfully asked me to put on. Thus, doubly blind, I was driven away. I was thrilled, apprehensive. I felt quite powerless, for in addition to everything else my costume was stiff and unyielding as though it hadn't been worn for a century and was rigid through lack of use. Yet there was no panic in me, for no sooner had we started than the servant in black said in a quiet voice: "I'm instructed to tell you, sir, that Clara is waiting for you with calmest joy." And those were the only words he would speak throughout the journey.

'Eventually,' said the little man through a mouthful of sausage-roll, 'I felt the carriage stop and the door open. "Now you may take off the blindfold," said my escort. I did so, and what a spectacle met my eyes! A country house with all its windows lit up. There were glimpses of a ballroom with people moving about beneath the twinkle of chandeliers. Liveried footmen were standing in the porte-cochère; one held my door for me as I climbed out in astonishment. Oh, I can't hope to convey to you here in broad daylight the magic which seized me that soft summer dusk before a great house sparkling with lights and breathing out its sound of chatter and the distant strains of music. Have you never felt at the same time happy and melancholy, not quite knowing what the moment means? The music I could hear was sad and remote. It spoke of all the things we've never had but still have managed to lose. How can that be? As I turned my head slightly I was no longer sure it was coming from the house. It took me a few moments to recognise my own *Carnaval*, the piece called "Chopin", but arranged for instruments. In its new disguise I found something missing from the piano original. It said to me: "You may never leave this place, Robert. Can't you feel its spell? Now you've been here and heard this music your life has already changed and your future begins anew." And just for an instant I shivered.

'In the doorway a lady was standing, waiting for me. She was dressed as though clasped with blossoms and wore a mask of petals. "I'm Columbine," she said, and I knew her voice as that of the woman in Harrods. "Welcome, Maestro," and she curtseyed slightly. "The night is yours. The house is also yours. And everyone in it is yours – for this one weekend. We are all masked. You alone are yourself, unmasked." "And Clara?" I asked. "How shall I know my Clara?" "How do we any of us know our Claras?" she replied. This was more enigmatic than helpful, I have to admit. But never mind – the excitement of it!

'I was shown into the ballroom and a footman announced in a loud voice: "Mr Robert Schumann!" I had yet to become a Doctor of Music, you see. At once a hush fell and the whole room turned towards me. And what a company it was! Everyone was in the most fantastic costumes, faces hidden behind masks which came down to just beneath their noses so they could eat and drink and . . . and *kiss*. It was very thrilling to me, quite sinister, especially their eyes, a wet glitter behind holes cut in metal and cardboard and cloth. Lady Columbine took me firmly by the wrist, led me over and introduced me to them one by one – "This is Pierrot; this is Harlequin; you really must get to know Estrella." They bowed and curtseyed and I noticed that one or two held my hand longer than was strictly necessary. And all the time I was wondering: Which one of them is my Clara? Is it she, with the small extra pressure of those gloved fingers? Or that one? Or that, with almost a child's teeth bared by her smile?

'Lady Columbine clapped her hands. "We shall all go through to the music room and, when our young maestro has collected himself after his long journey and these introductions, he will I hope play for us with his usual magic. From now on, the other world has ceased to exist." And at that moment, happening to glance through the french windows, I saw that the lights in the drive outside had been turned off, that the tall Rolls which had brought me had vanished, that nothing but darkness pressed up against the panes. Footmen now moved from window to window closing the shutters, drawing curtains, sealing the house. Yet all the time, from which room I couldn't tell, I seemed to hear the same melancholy tune I'd heard on my arrival. I never thought my own music could sound so wistful. Did you ever play that, dearest?' the little man broke off to ask my sister, who started as if in a trance. 'Did you ever play "Chopin"?'

'I've learned some Chopin,' said Caroline warily. 'Bits.'

'No, no, my "Chopin" from *Carnaval*.'

'Oh, that one. Yes, that's not too difficult. It's lovely. Really.'

All this while I had been aware of my father's unease. His silence was eloquent to us, as were his small movements which represented the tension of good manners struggling with anxiety about what this weird fellow would say next. The unbidden guest at our tablecloth had an oddly compelling way of speaking so that my father's reluctance to interrupt was understandable for reasons other than politeness. Even as I stared at the flakes of pastry caught among the patterns of the Fair Isle sweater I almost believed I, too, could hear distant music and see the costumed figures.

'Eventually,' the little man resumed, 'I sat down and played *Carnaval*. I played without music, of course. Two tall candles stood on either side shedding their soft yellow glow. It was a remarkable instrument and I did things that night I'd never done before, found things in my own music I hadn't known were there. As I reached "Chopin" a sigh went around as if at last everyone was hearing what until then had been only half heard, not quite audible. And I knew that none of us there would ever forget it.

'When I'd finished the whole work everyone was all over me, I can tell you. I'm not being immodest. I never bettered that performance and I doubt that anybody ever has. Servants went around with champagne and bon-bonnières containing little sugared balls which had a positively magical effect on us. Sated with music, we all began to sparkle. I can't remember the dishes I ate, the glasses I drank, not even – I have to say it – the lips I kissed. For how else was I to find my Clara? She was there somewhere, that divine child; I could feel her presence all the time I was playing. The house was full of her elusiveness, mask upon mask upon mask. I pursued her all over it, from one dark bedroom to another, in closet and passageway, in attic and on back staircase. And after each encounter – no! Exquisite, but that wasn't her. A little too old, a fraction too knowing, not completely sincere about the music . . . *My* music, which after all must have gone straight to her heart.

'Time no longer existed. For all I knew day had long since dawned outside the shuttered windows, midday come and gone, another night fallen. There was nothing in the world but the golden pursuit of masked figures and all the while this faint music. Until finally, in a forgotten servant's room in a disused wing, I came to the end of my search. From behind the door I could hear her voice, a child's voice since she was barely thirteen, singing my haunting melody. I – '

' – wonder if you'd like a cup of tea?' my father broke in, getting to his feet and pulling the thermos out of the basket. 'And then I suppose we'd better think about a move. The traffic, you know. The Leatherhead by-pass especially.' His firm, professional voice and the sound of Bakelite and unscrewing and pouring tore us back to a normality which felt most peculiar. The little man was rocking mutely on his birch stump, red in the face with the agitation of his story. There was a feeling that something awful had been headed off in the nick of time.

'So,' said my father, handing him a mug of tea, 'do you still compose, Dr Schumann?'

'Oh . . . oh, thank you. Oh yes, yes, I do. The tunes won't let me alone.'

Sympathy must have prompted my sister's surprising intervention. 'I'd like to learn some of your new pieces so long as they're not too difficult,' she said encouragingly. I noticed she was gripping the toe of my father's shoe.

The little man turned on her the most extraordinary, wrenched smile while the tea trickled unheeded from his tilted cup on to his already stained trousers. 'Why, yes,' he cried. 'My dearest one, I've searched for you high and low to give you them. My Clara.'

It was an instant which froze us all. I remember the thick thrill in my stomach when I saw the tears run down the little man's face. This was the moment for my father to interpose decisively; yet again it was my sister who seemed more capable of a reasonable response, as if she were touched rather than frightened by the stranger's pathetic charm.

'I'm afraid my name isn't Clara,' she told him. 'Awfully sorry.'

'Not Clara?' he whispered.

'No. I'm Caroline.'

'Caroline.' He stared at a clump of bracken. 'But it nearly contains her. The anagram, you see. One letter short. So nearly. Always so nearly.' He dried his face with his sweater. 'Never mind. These days it's getting late and you're a dear, sweet child and a pianist as well so I want you to have them.'

He began to wrestle in his trousers, tugging at a pocket. An object flew out and landed rattling in the middle of the tablecloth but the man's attention was on the crumpled pages he had found. He smoothed them and we could see music manuscript with notes and staves.

'There,' he said, now on his feet and handing them down to my sister with an archaic bow. I wondered for a moment if he would kiss her hand but he became distracted by the lost object my father was holding out to him. 'Ah, my bonbonnière,' he said with a dire wink. 'Thank you, doctor.'

I had recognised it at once as a pillbox: one of those circular off-white affairs made of pleated waxed paper. You don't see them nowadays. My father had given its label a knowing glance and now said, 'You might perhaps take one, Mr Pinckney?' But something in the little man's mood had broken for he only repeated: 'Never mind, it's getting late,' before muttering 'It's been charming. Quite like old times,' while hurrying away without a backward glance, head bent, his awful sweater quickly lost among the dapples of the tree trunks.

Nobody said much as we rapidly repacked the picnic things. All I could register was an eleven-year-old's certainty that we would never be coming back to this spot. Other ghosts had taken the place of my mother's. On the way back to the car my father took a short cut across the flank of a wooded hill which suddenly afforded us an unexpected downward view. In the middle distance stood a grim Victorian pile from one of whose outbuildings rose a brick smokestack like that of a steam laundry. He paused.

'And that, I fear, is the magical country house.'

Once we were safely back in the car I asked, 'Was he mad?'

'Rather off his chump, I'd say,' came the diagnosis.

'But harmless really,' said Caroline.

'No doubt,' said my father with a fretful smile. 'No doubt.'

The pages the little man had presented to her seemed nowhere to be found and for some time there was nothing tangible to remind us our haunted picnic. Months later they turned up in the AA book; Caroline must have dropped them into the Wolseley's door pocket. The crotchets and quavers were indecipherable; the crude, aching drawings were not.

All this was long ago, of course, and now our father, too, is dead. Certain of his details are already slipping away. But to this day when Caroline can be persuaded to play *Carnaval* the music at once brings back an intense memory of faces sliding one behind the other – our mother, our father, the little man and his sad fantastic company, all moving in that far-off summer glade with the unease of an inexhaustible longing. Our yearnings, it seems, express us more memorably than do our compromised equanimities. The piece called 'Chopin' has a particular effect on Caroline. She once described it as claiming an unfair intimacy, like being made love to in public by a perfect stranger.

Jaro

HE HAD BEEN leaning against the *Aperto/Chiuso* sign at the entrance to the filling-station and now hovered diffidently on the forecourt as the Agip man rummaged in his greasy satchel for change, sidling up rapidly at the last moment and speaking through the open window on the passenger's side.

'You're not going towards Manciano? Even a kilometre?'

He looked all in. Sixteen, seventeen, ratty blond hair; beaky, with the bones of a sparrow. Clearly foreign but speaking good Italian. He sank into the seat and momentarily closed his eyes, let his mouth sag enough to show greenish teeth. His clothes exhaled.

'You're not really going to Manciano, are you?' he asked with weary canniness. 'But anything's better than walking.' He had crusts the colour of breadcrumbs in the corners of his eyes. 'My cousin might be there.'

With unexpected formality he turned and offered a thin, dirty hand as the car gathered speed. He was called Jaro; said he was from Croatia, somewhere up not far from

Trieste. Maybe this explained his fluency in Italian. But then he gave an account of wandering for eight months in Italy, eight months looking for scattered remnants of his family, living on scraps of information passed on by other refugees, titbits of hope which were less useful than kindly meant in an ironic sort of way. He had, it seemed, an instinctive aversion to authorities of any kind. Whosever mercy he would throw himself on, it would not be that of official charity, still less that of men and women in uniform.

'You don't understand,' he flatly said, hunched by the window and watching Umbria pass with an indifferent eye. 'Confidence? What do you mean?' (for efforts were being made by the Italian authorities to keep some sort of track of illegal immigrants, though it was always less trouble to pick up Africans and Arabs and ask for their papers than it was to pester blonds). 'What do you mean, have confidence in you? Why care what I think of you? It's good to be taken somewhere near Manciano if it's not out of your way. That's all.' Unexpectedly he flipped down the sun visor and stared at himself in the vanity mirror.

Wherever Manciano was it was a good few kilometres off. He accepted with equanimity the car's stopping by a group of houses at the roadside, and whatever suspicion had sparked behind his derelict child's mask was swamped at once by the smell inside the pizzeria. The pizzas came sliding out by the shovelful from a blazing brick hole in the wall, their bubbles of puddled cheese adding a savoury layer to the ambient scent of hot dough. Jaro ate three without stopping, later bringing out with him in a cardboard box the uneaten two-thirds of another. When not actually eating he had spent a long time in the little washroom, to the inconvenience of several patrons who were obliged to keep returning to their tables and continue scowling and plucking at their fingers with napkins. Jaro now climbed back into the car with a certain bounce and immediately examined himself again in the mirror on the sun visor. He had washed his hair in the sink, evidently, for it hung limply in damp clots and smelt of the peppermint-scented soap found in motorway washroom dispensers. The crusts had gone. The whitish rime around his mouth had been replaced by a fresh orange moustache from the cans of Fanta he'd drunk. He wiped this away with a clean linen napkin plainly just stolen from the pizzeria.

'Mean bastards,' he observed, flipping up the visor. 'No soap in the washroom, can you imagine? Only a titchy basin and no soap. No problem, though. You just carry a condom of liquid soap and keep refilling it, did you know that? The things you learn.'

Post-pizza Jaro was a more expansive creature, though still not entirely relaxed. Enough had happened in his short life to convince him that free lunches weren't. At least he evidently felt enough grim confidence to tackle the matter head-on. He was sometimes given lifts by people with intentions of their own, he said. He particularly remembered some German or Austrian who'd picked him up outside Bolzano a month or two ago in an olive-green BMW.

'The car was really *hot* inside. He had the heating turned up like a greenhouse. He drove out of town fast until we came to this deserted lay-by on the edge of a wood. Snow everywhere and this deep black forest off to the right. It was late afternoon and getting dark and the cars were passing us with their sidelights on. There weren't many of them. I hadn't eaten for two days, got these soaking feet like lumps of wet ice. So the old sod tries it on, shifting around in this squeaky leather jacket on the squeaky leather seat. On and on he goes till he starts getting really pissed off that I can't get a hard-on. In the end he throws me out and drives off – *rawrr!* – in a great spray of snow all red from the tail lights.'

Odd for its interpolated detail and sound effects, this little story was told without apparent grudge. It was entirely up to the listener to fill in whatever blanks as the still frozen, hungry, homeless child was left standing at the forest's edge as punishment for his cancelled libido. What cheerless landscape was this, with war raging somewhere over the horizon and disbanded families straggling across alien territory like hibernating ants burnt out of a hollow tree? Just Europe at the twentieth century's end, as at its beginning and middle. Jaro had walked to the next town because no-one else would stop, not on a darkening road with snow coming down and a mass of shopping to do before the hypermarket closed. – You couldn't blame them – he seemed to be saying. – There's no connection between one person's life and any other's. People wander in and out of our field of vision, some smiling and some limping. Even their own kids are unrecognisable in the wrong light. –

Shortly after he had told this story the car was held up for what seemed like hours at a set of temporary traffic lights marking roadworks. In the interval Jaro fell asleep, head sagging back against the window and mouth open. Among the furred teeth a few neat fillings were visible which, like a certain mannerliness, suggested a quite underelict past. Once the lights had changed Manciano appeared a couple of kilometres down the road. He was not easily woken. In barely ten minutes his face had taken on the crushed shapelessness of an infant's.

'Manciano,' he repeated uncomprehendingly at the window as if the view of outskirts it offered ought to mean something to him. His eyelids kept drooping. Apparently his cousin should be here somewhere but there was no address. Would it be too much to ask at the police station for him? The post office? The town hall? If Jaro himself went he might be detained or worse. 'Trust me,' he said pleadingly. 'I'll write his name for you. Please. Can't I stay here just for a bit? You can take the car keys with you. And remove the radio if you want, and anything else.' He was asleep before the door closed on him.

Predictably, Manciano gave up not the smallest shred of evidence of a cousin, a refugee or even a foreigner – not unless (as someone in the Town Hall remarked) you counted the Tunisian *vu cumprà* who pushed his pram about town on Tuesdays and Fridays selling Biros, quartz watches and Bic lighters. 'Friend of a friend?' said a *carabiniere* in a way which hinted at illicit flirtations. 'Better try the hotel. It's in the square. Why not come back if you have no luck there?'

A fruitless hour thus passed, at the end of which the car was still there and so was the sleeping Jaro who didn't even wake as the door opened, the engine started, the road flowed back beneath the tyres. Manciano had indeed been a detour and it was some time before the car slowed to drive across a bridge of railway sleepers and along a track edged by olive terraces. It stopped outside a small farmhouse. A dog barked a greeting from the end of a chain. Doves sat in a glimmering row on the garage roof, outlined against the dusk. After repeated shakings Jaro opened his eyes. The courtesy light revealed them full of the tears squeezed out by dreams.

'I bet this is your house, right?'

Once inside, in the brick-floored kitchen with the brick-lined ceiling from whose rafters hung bunches of this and that, he said, 'But you live here *alone*? No family? No children?' His eyes were quite round now, empty of sleep. They contained a child's intense curiosity about families, possibly tinged with an orphaned wistfulness. He quickly lit on the photograph hanging by the door. 'Your son? Where is he now? Why America? He looks my age.' Then the doubt, verging on suspicion. 'Is Luca really your son?' His unresting prowl and his questions filled the kitchen with a sense of disintegration, as though the sole purpose of people known and loved was to be forever doubted, separated, dispersed. It was only when the dog came in and took excitedly to this sour-clothed wanderer that the atmosphere began to knit itself together again. On the floor by the fire they sprawled over each other in a meltdown of puppification. The only thing which could distract Jaro was the prospect of a bath while supper cooked. In the bedroom assigned him (which had a heavy round-topped door like that of an ancient chapel) drawers were opened and rummaged through for suitable clothes. 'Good old Luca,' he said with a flawed smile and vanished into the bathroom.

He reappeared in the kitchen after nearly an hour, heralded by wafts of myosotis, wearing clean jeans and a T-shirt. The beak of his nose was very pink, adding vulnerability to its prominence. Adolescence had pushed it out ahead of the laggardly rest of him. His teeth were distinctly whiter. Scoured and renewed, he moved about with the confidence of one who has regained the persona his own mother might have recognised.

'There's a guitar on the wall upstairs,' he said. 'It's been put up at an angle so it must be an ornament.'

This was well observed. Taking the chastened silence for permission Jaro left and returned with it. He blew the dust off and peered inside.

'You don't play, do you? And I'll bet Luca doesn't, either. Look, it comes from Valencia. Oh, the strings are dried out. I don't know if they'll stand tuning.'

He sat on the raised hearth and, as the roasting chicken poppled and spat quietly in the oven, tuned the guitar. As he did so his nose, impendent above the instrument, began to lose its appendage-like awkwardness and turn instead into a delicate sense organ, sniffing at the notes as they rose.

'That's A,' he said at last, satisfied. 'You don't believe me. Trust me, that's A. Now we can get bottom E and top E.' A blond lock of hair dangled as he bent further over, listening to the harmonics beating. Despite his intentness the tuning filled the kitchen with an unpropitious sound, the nasal whangings of notes sliding up and down at their pegs' adjustment, the *plunk-plunk-plunk* of repetition. It all seemed to herald the kind of tedium which promised to stretch illimitably ahead until it infected the very stones of the house. That was until Jaro's hands took the place of his nose as his best feature. Most hands remain little better than paws but sometimes the unlikeliest hand becomes transfigured the instant it closes around a chisel, kneads dough, touches an instrument. Jaro's fingers now had no connection with the row of grubby digits which had mutely gripped the car's windowsill in the filling station. These were fingers happily at home on familiar territory and all at once, after the briefest pause, they began to play.

The music was startlingly loud in the kitchen,

absolutely arresting in its presence and immediacy in a way which made a mockery of the record industry's claims to their products' lifelike fidelity. There was no substitute for the real thing; and Jaro was the real thing. – Listen – said his fingers – this is who I am. The rest is anonymous flotsam. –

'Very bad,' he said delightedly at the end. 'My hands are too stiff. It's been so long. That was supposed to be a study by Fernando Sor but my teacher wouldn't have recognised it. And these old gut strings of yours are useless. They've lost their resonance.'

Over supper he withdrew a little. Or rather, he wouldn't be obedient in his answers. He was from the Istrian peninsula, from near Fiume (which d'Annunzio and his Fascists had annexed in the early Twenties) and his guitar teacher lived in Zagreb but was a Slovene. Or something like that. Now was not the time to try and make sense of Balkan ethnic divisions. Jaro wouldn't talk at all about his family but became intent on his food as questions about mothers and fathers and siblings hung sadly in the air. Instead he offered more stories from the last eight months' odyssey, full of the hangdog wisdom of marginal living whose subtext of time-wasting was swamped by the rococo energy of youth. He told of ferocious urchins encamped on wastelands around the great cities of Milan and Bologna, professional thieves of nine and ten indentured to gangsters and too young to be prosecuted. They had been filtering steadily down from the Balkans years before Yugoslavia fell apart. He told of sleeping in sheds and barns and begging food and running from vicious dogs; of being shot at by a nervous farmer in the foothills of the Alps. He spoke of talismans: of passports and *carte d'identità* and work permits (in the back pocket of his sour trousers had been a valid driver's licence – clearly stolen – belonging to someone in Parma).

'You know, that's the best meal I've had for months,' he said when he could eat no more. He was thin enough that, like a puppy's, his stomach beneath the T-shirt made a tight dome. There was nothing uncivil in this form of thanks: it was more a token of naturalness as of a boy in his own kitchen. Refusing coffee as he'd refused all but a single glass of white wine, Jaro reached once more for the guitar which had attracted his avid glances throughout the meal. Again he played the piece by Sor, this time with more confidence, listening with head on one side instead of watching his fingers on the frets. The house did not yet have electricity and a quality in the lamp- or firelight fleetingly made visible the man of sixty he might turn into, or maybe revealed a grandparent in his blood. The beaky profile became for that moment immensely refined, the hollowed eyes contemplative, the set of head and shoulder alert with habitual listening. Finishing the study he switched immediately into an altogether lengthier piece, melodious, vaguely Mozartean and initially of a haunting plangency. It ended with a lightweight rondo whose figurations became more complex at each repeat of the merry theme. Jaro threw it off with such panache that his occasional fluffs only added to the music's vividness.

'I'm so stiff,' he mourned with pleasure. 'Really rusty. It took ages to learn that and now see what's happened in a few months. I was going to play to a professor in Zagreb but the war . . . Oh, it's a sonata by Mauro Giuliani. He was a Bolognese but lived in Vienna. Something like that. My teacher says he was the greatest guitar virtuoso of his day. Even Beethoven admired him.'

But in the silence which stretched on after these remarks a listlessness began to creep in such as to leave the music hanging in the air like a reproach. The ear went on hearing the final chords' brightness but the echoes they had set up were more persistent and more dark. They hollowed out the kitchen until everything – the lamplight, the meal, the sense of rescue, even the music's dazzling tinsel – were left afloat and tiny above gulfs of wastage and despair. It might all have been discharged by a sudden outburst of tears, a collapse into comfortings. But the boy's refusal to break merely hardened the outlines of whatever had stalked in. Even the dog, which had slept throughout the music, groaned and raised its head towards the door. The malign intruder spoke out of the firelight and from among the echoes. It reminded that small tranquil moments, snatched pleasures, even affection itself, are always under-lain by the iron indifference on whose surface they float as beatific scum.

All too evidently Jaro also heard this voice. In Italian,

one doesn't sing for one's supper, one merely earns it. He now said quietly, mockingly, still holding the guitar: 'Well, did I earn my supper? Or don't I stop there?' The contemplative elder he might (if he survived) become had entirely vanished. Nothing now sat on the hearth but street trash wearing someone else's clothes.

Tiredness, of course, that would account for everything. The boy was stone weary. He stumbled upstairs into his room with a gas camping lamp, still clutching the guitar. The heavy door closed firmly like that of an abbot on a pastoral visit to a nunnery. Uneasy silence fell. The house tensed around his unseen presence as if expecting to hear, in the depths of the night, a muffled crying or the terrified howls of re-lived atrocity. But there was only, before sleep, a half-hearted attempt at the Beatles' 'Hey, Jude'. Sometimes when a cock has its throat cut and just before its last energy drains out it will try feebly to crow. This desolate sound is not a last attempt at defiance so much as the mere noise of the creature running down, its own programmed voice, as unvolitional as a rose's scent as it lies on a bonfire. Such was Jaro's 'Hey, Jude' behind his oak barrier in the darkness.

And now came brisk blue weather, a handful of days the colour of reprieve. He moved about in the sunlight carrying the guitar which had long since passed into his possession. The two were inseparable. 'It got stolen, didn't it?' was his answer to the obvious question, since it had become impossible to imagine him fleeing a war without rescuing his own instrument. 'The bastards just took it': less actual people than agents of that perpetual corrosion which had seeped up from below and leached it away.

The struggle within Jaro took on a stark clarity in the bright air of the terraces. The drifting orphan longing for a home was pitted against the survivor who knew it was fatal to risk the certainty of renewed loss. The nostalgias can't have helped: the oil-lit farmhouse, the long rows of vines strung between posts stained blue-green with generations of copper solution. 'Aren't you going to prune the olives this year?' he asked. 'It's nearly April.' And for a moment a vaguely similar terrain hovered over Umbria, an Istria with its own olives and vines and bucolic rhythms. It had spoken for him unawares, and memory clouded his face while he attacked the guitar with a fearsome outburst of scales and arpeggios. In similar fashion he took care to avoid physical contact, except that now and then a betraying hand would reach out instinctively. These lapses were always well punished with aloof withdrawal to somewhere slightly conspicuous such as the rusty iron saddle of an abandoned Fiat tractor, an antique which it was easy to imagine hadn't moved since the 1950s. He would sit perched up high, outlined as a lonely huddle with a guitar, ploughing off motionlessly through docks and nettles to nowhere imaginable.

It couldn't go on, of course. At some point charity has to

shade into commitment or else turn away and reward other victims for their pitiability. And commitment means a life upheaved, griefs and horrors of every kind with no outcome guaranteed except, in the absence of the most rigorous undeception, a bog of conflicting longings and meshing disappointments. The confusion of someone else wearing Luca's clothes and playing Luca's guitar was already painful. 'Don't mother me!' came Jaro's voice from those clothes, sitting on the tractor or on a step among irises, always at a distance but never – never quite – out of sight. 'That's the trouble with you women. You never can let us be.' And in between, snatches of Bach, fragments of Villa-Lobos, riffs of a demonic Jimi Hendrix; the outcries of a drowning talent all at sea among styles as among desires, among alternative futures wasting away beyond a succession of horizons.

The agent of precipitation – and it might have been anything – was probably Francesco, calling on his way home with a bundle of mail which the postman couldn't deliver since his moped was lying dead in a ditch. He arrived capless but in uniform in a car which, although it wasn't actually marked *Carabinieri*, did bear a number plate prefixed by the military's red letters 'EI'. He was whistling as he got out, waved a hand and called 'Buon giorno' towards Jaro and his guitar before handing over the letters with his usual pleasantries and driving away again. Thought about retrospectively, Francesco's very friendliness must have fed Jaro's anxiety about betrayal.

When viewed as a possible lover, what local cop mightn't be curious about strangers on familiar premises? Or be slow to winkle out details about vagrants with stolen driving licences? (even though the licence, together with the trousers, had been burned the day after Jaro's arrival).

'Oh yes,' said the boy sarcastically, 'you told him I was a cousin from up north somewhere. A likely tale.' And he remained quite unchastened when reminded that it was no more unlikely than his own tale of a cousin in Manciano. The Manciano relative had been a safety net whereas this was conspiracy. Reassurances were useless, as were remarks beginning 'Sooner or later' and dealing with coming in from the cold and resuming guitar lessons under whoever was the nearest thing to Segovia that Italy could currently offer. That night for the first time he drank quite a lot of wine and showed signs, before being headed off, of becoming ineptly amorous, though probably only to pay the policeman back. More suggested was the child who badgers to be allowed to make a chocolate cake, but who loses interest in the absurd gulf of time which separates his greed from the finished article and is reduced to licking the uncooked mixture off the bowl before wandering away.

The next morning, without a sound from the dog, he had gone, taking a few more clothes and – of course – the one uncontaminated companion he could talk to, listen to and trust, who was attuned to his own perfect pitch. It seemed both officious and offensive to go driving around the lanes and highways looking for a youth with a guitar; only later would his departure take on aspects of deliverance. At first it left guilt and the rawness of pity, much intensified by the discovery that on his last night Jaro had wet the bed. Unaccustomed alcohol? The deep anaesthesia of misery? Meanwhile the dog roamed the rooms looking for whatever had been and then gone, leaving a house shaking with the echoes of illimitable damage and with the ghost of a guitar on one wall.

Anxieties of Desire

THAT A MUSICIAN should be haunted by sounds seems
only proper; that they should have been the sounds
peculiar to his exile is equally right. They come to me in
my memory as frontier noises, for the outskirts of Algiers
in the early 1930s formed a frontier between city and
desert, modern and ancient. My nearest muezzin had
perfect pitch: five times a day he began his melismas
unfailingly on E♭, varying the chants with improvisatory
flourishes of his own. At dawn the sound would rise,
richly decorated and trembling against the eggshell sky
like a single peacock feather. Soon afterwards the copper
beaters began work in the souk. At night, sounds of
violence and travel. Every few weeks the police would
round up the stray dogs which slunk in from the desert's
fringes, herd them into my alley and shoot them more or
less accurately as a measure against rabies. The snarling
and shrieking and gunshots were terrifying; and even
though the corpses were immediately thrown into carts to
be burned the alley was always black with vultures next
morning, pecking at stains and gulping fragments. Most

nights, though, long after the radio and flutes had stopped in the little café whose name I can't now remember, that silence fell which is, as Mozart observed, the most beautiful thing in music. It was the voice of a wilderness which began only a couple of streets away. Sometimes in those still hours I would hear a caravan arrive as though on tiptoe, the velvet shuffle of camels and a tinkling like loose change.

Had I not committed myself to strange territory? I was a thorough European on both parental sides, born in Antwerp, raised largely in Berlin and attending the Paris Conservatoire (Prix de Rome, 1922, for *Les Jardins Mystérieux*). What had such a man to do with deserts and muezzins? What had I known of Algiers, except that Saint-Saëns had died there of a fever? Well, it's a shocking enough story for it shows that the muses, far from being the handmaidens of high art and encouragers of those prepared to sacrifice a life in their service, are in reality traitorous hags, as fickle as schoolgirls and of an equally brainless cunning.

You too, perhaps, hypocrite reader? You who have just reached down your damned encyclopaedia and found – aha! – that in 1922 the Prix de Rome was *not awarded*. Oh yes it was; but it was taken away again from me by the vilest imaginable machinations. The spectacle of those academicians – whose vellum scalps sported withered laurel in place of hair – snarling like curs behind the iron gates of their own entrenched opinions was more than an artist could bear. Normally ponderous professors scuttered about, robes flapping, marshalling votes and writing malicious squibs to members of rival cliques. Never had the Académie so humiliated itself in disharmony. And why? Because my beautiful *Jardins* were too unfashionable for it, too *mystérieux*, too talented. I had failed to put into them enough evidence of the professors' own teaching. These academics didn't want strange scents and uncanny perspectives. They wanted heavy hints that behind the delicate colours was a technique like pumice, something grey and hard left over from the volcanoes of a former age. Not a set-piece canon, maybe, but at least some thoroughgoing counterpoint in the orchestra, a mock-learned and witty fugato (say) while the singers wailed earnestly on. Anyway, as all the world knows my piece became a *cause célèbre*. The jury of nine composers gave a six-to-three verdict in *Jardins'* favour, those from the Institut being unanimous. Then, thanks to vicious lobbying on the part of my detractors – including, I later discovered, approaches to the illustrious J-J – the Académie vetoed it. So: no performance of the work that October; no four years' government pension: no residence in the Villa Medici. Very well, then, so be it. None so deaf as those who will not hear! I turned my back on them all, the so-called musical establishment, those tight little circles of dullards and perverts who simply played each other's works and sniffed each other's farts and gave each other fawning reviews. In any case, who ever heard again of any winner of the Prix de Rome? Debussy, Massenet, Bizet, Gounod . . . Four real composers. That's about it for a prize which has been awarded annually (or not) ever since 1803. René Martens, then, was a name destined to rise from ranks other than these.

The wilderness: that's where all true artists go to lick their wounds and recover their strength in order to return like lions. Even as I headed for it, not knowing where it was, I moved about Europe, a job here, a job there. If there is such a crime as puellicide I came close to committing it on many occasions as I sat listening to some hapless child with plaits and freckles massacring a Bach Two-Part Invention. But I learned to congeal. Coolly I told them I wasn't paid to hear them practise but to hear them play. Like ice I took the envelope left for me on the brass salver in the hall. Slowly the lions' breath entered me, undeniable, thrilling as strychnine. My paws itched. All this while I was working, studying, scribbling and tearing up, swallowing and swallowing pride and feeling it gradually turn to the breath of lions down among lights and bowels. René Martens was biding his time. I think now he was shucking off the Conservatoire and replacing it with more Teutonic influences from his Berlin adolescence. That tradition certainly supplied heartening examples of composers pacing themselves, making themselves prowl their cages. Bruckner was over forty before he began his list of great symphonies; Brahms didn't complete his own First until he was forty-three. This was fit company for René Martens. The essence of desire is waiting.

Yet just as it had taken Brahms so long to learn how to step from the dense shadow which Beethoven cast, so it took me most of my wandering thirties to overcome Paris's pernicious hold. If I'd heard it once, I'd heard it a thousand times when I was a student: 'But the symphony is dead, Monsieur Martens. It belongs to another age' (the elegantly cocked eyebrow, the dismissive flutter of the hand). Oh how I wish I could have cast Messiaen in their teeth at the time. Young Olivier did the right thing, of course: all those first prizes at the Conservatoire in the late 1920s – harmony and counterpoint, fugue, improvisation and organ playing, composition . . . But we're all different and we have to run our own courses. Mine turned me into the lone and humble student of my own academy. I hired and borrowed instruments, made myself passably competent on several. Never again would I write a non-existent note for a French horn – the occasion, I remember, for quite exaggerated scorn and calumny on the part of one of *Jardins'* savagers. Hadn't the young Schumann made just such an error in the very first bar of his very first symphony, *The Spring*? Genius goes where it has to and is sometimes careless of details in the overwhelming rush of inspiration.

Slowly I fell away to the south. I ran my tongue around Vienna for left-over pockets of musical sweetness, sucked at Florence for its lingering taste of blood and brilliance,

swept the streets of Rome for useful dust (such handsome
little Fascists!). While there I would make a point of passing
the Villa Medici at a mocking lope, regal with scorn and
disdain, wondering what pampered and cosseted expat-
riate wunderkind was holed up behind the tall shutters,
making a bid for Parnassus at French taxpayers' expense.
And I . . . I was free of such things! Thank God! And so at
length I reached Algiers, having run innumerable gaunt-
lets of whining creditors, prurient landladies and miffed
policemen. I arrived with a growing bundle of score
beneath my arm, needing only a neutral African sun to
shine on the completion of that first, great symphony of
mine.

So it was that the tawny breath of the Sahara scorched into
me like big cats at my back as I sat in a whitewashed room
and wrote while five times a day the muezzin shook his
peacock feathers in the rectangle of sky. The café's flutes
and wailing radio, the metal beaters and even the shot dogs
are there in the score for anyone to hear, while the slow
movement's tread is the velvety pad of camels bearing
from unimaginable lands strange and disquieting bounty.
It was, in fact, to this very movement that I was adding a
late inspiration, an intermittent soft jingling like harness
buffed by windblown sand, when I happened to catch
sight of a copy of *Le Mercure du Sud*. Normally I barely
glanced at the Arts page, at those syndicated reports of
the distant, parochial goings-on in the world's so-called

artistic capital. If one deigned to notice them in all their lickspittle pretension it could only mean one felt excluded – and you surely know me well enough by now to realise the absurdity of that idea. I was all too happy to be working my work, free at last of a metropolis which, like a child, considered herself both the universe and its centre. Yet on this occasion glance I did. There beneath the headline '*Début éclatant*' was an account of the dazzling première of René Martens' First Symphony.

My instant reaction was a thrill of joy. At last, you pigs! *Now* will you . . . ? before thought overtook it like a javelin, piercing it through the heart. Feverishly I read the piece, bewildered, aghast. René Martens had last Sunday himself conducted the first performance of his symphony. L'Orchestre de Paris had given a sumptuous account of a work which, from that moment, had become the talk of Europe. No lesser laureates than Poulenc and Milhaud had hailed it as the most original, most beautiful, most . . . Beyond the window the muezzin hit his usual smug E♭; I flung the paper from me, at him, at the world, at Allah. It fluttered through the aperture and vanished. A donkey added its tortured mockery from the alley below. *There was another René Martens*. I couldn't believe it. I clung to the table. Once more, by some malignant joke which the muses must have hatched in helpless stitches, my success had been stolen from me. My very name had been stolen from me. I could have believed a jealous rival had crept in by night, taken my score off the table, had published it under his own name.

That night the curs were culled again. I lay awake on my mat, staring at the flickering ceiling with a snarl so fixed it ached, hearing the bullets crash through skulls and brains, ribs and hearts, seeing the stranger who had stolen my life die a thousand times over. It was his body I heard tossed again and again into the cart until it rolled off the heap and had to be stuffed ignominiously behind the tailboard. Trundled to the edge of the desert, this huge stack of the fake René Martens was doused in waste oil and piled around with his spurious manuscript. A match flared, the orange flames leapt up and sent heavy, stinking smoke into the absolving African night. How his fat sputtered and melted, dripping blue flames into the sand! How his brains bubbled and seethed! How his internal gases expanded until slowly he raised himself to a sitting position, blackened arms seared into an imploring boxer's defence, puny against an obliterating blow! And how, released by the cleansing flames, his crotchets and quavers and bar lines took grateful wing, fluttered upwards and were lost for ever. Oh, I lay awake that night; and never once did I take my eyes off the play of those distant orange flames on my chamber wall; and never once did my grin cease until wearily I sat up and kneaded my face back into an expression fit to meet dawn's light and the world of human commerce.

Sayeeda on her splayed ankles couldn't bring me coffee hot enough, thick enough, bitter enough. I cursed her puny brazier and cheeseparing ways, hurried off through the souk and via a succession of mewing and sullen cafés was fortified until my heart raced and ears sang. Normally I avoided Le P'tit Panthéon, that predictable outpost of fart-sniffers, but today it would serve me by having copies of all the major Paris newspapers, flown over from Marseilles in a rickety Latécoère which honked and wallowed outside the harbour twice a week like a tubercular goose. The papers were there. Three of them carried reports of the concert, one of the columns included a photograph of 'the composer'. My hand was shaking too violently for his features to be legible so I dropped the paper on the table and stared. My usurper was shockingly young, which accorded with a description of him as twenty-one. This was awful. A sharply intelligent, good-looking – no, no, I was able to revise this as soon as it was thought. He reminded me – got it! – of the young Mendelssohn, a certain Hebraic cast . . . *Flashy* good looks, then, shall we allow? A drop of sweat fell from the tip of my impendent nose and obliterated this other René Martens with scribbles of reversed print bleeding through from the back of the page.

What to do? We biders-in-the-wilderness have our resources. Over the years I had regularly practised callisthenics and to these exercises I turned now. With a vengeance, one might say. I had never allowed myself to fall into that trap of degeneracy which sucks at and claims so many artists. With flour paste I stuck the photograph of the toast of Paris to my chamber wall so he was forced to watch the ominous intent as I drove my body inexorably towards physical superiority.

Meanwhile, of course, it wouldn't have done to allow this fellow to get on top of me so I wrote him a perfectly graceful letter in which I enquired if he was aware that he had a rather older and better established namesake? He had only to ask around the Conservatoire and *l'affaire Martens* would assuredly be recalled, not least by Maître F— and Professeur de Faculté H. E., together with their testimonials to my singleminded career. (For never make the mistake of thinking that because one isn't constantly there, impertinently beating on their gates, the figures of the establishment don't know of one's existence. They know, all right, just as the firelit circle of roistering tribesmen knows that at their backs, beyond the bonhomie and the furthest reach of the flickering light, prowls the lion.)

In due time I received a reply: civil, though not – I thought – over-respectful, saying that he had of course no idea there was another René Martens who composed. ('Who composed' was cheeky. He made it sound like a hobby.) Further, he claimed, nobody at the Conservatoire whom he had asked could remember an *affaire Martens*, while F— and H. E. had both been dead for years. (It was an obvious pretence never to have heard of either of them.) However, he ended, he was sure there was room in the world for two composers named Martens, given that there were about thirty-three called Bach. In any case (oh, breezy and winsome puppy!) mightn't we agree to turn the situation to our advantage? If ever we wrote something which displeased our respective publics we could always claim 'that other fellow' had written it . . . And so signed off with a flourish.

The muezzin sang. There was not a moment to be lost. The muezzin sang again. All moments were equally lost and had been from the beginning. Better to beat out copper pots all day than attempt to make a new music, practise an old art. I forced myself back to my poor symphony. The score was dog-eared. The opening pages had a weary, travel-stained look to them. I'm not ashamed to say I wept at my table for many hours, re-living the sundry defeats and hardships of a life which had, after all, been undertaken for nothing but the greater glory of art, in celebration of beauty, without a thought for self-advancement. Could a man of my talents *not* have advanced himself had he chosen the easy road of wooing the public? Naturally he could. And why hadn't he chosen that road? Because that sort of success was too easy, too flimsy. One had to work hard in order to be as unsuccessful with the public as I, a truly finished composer in private. So be it, then. I would at last begin my public career.

Even I, in my distress and anxiety to hear my symphony, to promote its glories, could see that another First Symphony by a second René Martens (although of course really the first) would be a little hard for that public to take. When in tears a despairing father goes upstairs to remove his beloved infant's life with a straight razor, he does so with no less murderous mercy than mine as I surgically extracted my symphony's slow movement. I made a fair copy, added a title ('Tone Poem: *Nuits Mauresques*') and sent it to a good acquaintance in Berlin, Count Shuker d'Iffni, with the request that he place it as soon as possible with Peters or Breitkopf in Leipzig, or similar reputable house. This, I felt sure, would cook this little Hebrew's goose for him. It is easy enough to be a big frog in the little pond that is French music, but German music is what counts, as everyone acknowledges.

When these publishers rejected the work I was at first incredulous. On thinking about it further I assumed there might well be an angle to this which I, in my innocence, hadn't considered. Despite the best efforts of Germany's leaders at the time, members of this other Martens' tribe still reached their tentacles into the most diverse concerns – the arts, sciences, banking – and music publishing was clearly no exception. I wrote again to the Count, warning him to consider this probability and to use his best offices to ensure my score reached only men of unimpeachable reliability, *or else* . . . Of course I never wrote 'or else'; but there are ways and ways whereby someone who is light on his feet need not laboriously spell things out. This Count, this Shuker d'Iffni, was someone I had known here in Algiers. I believe his title was genuine enough, as, presumably, his fortune. He had lorded it in a huge crenellated villa in the hills – a lot of very young, willowy servants, a well-known enthusiasm for photography, need I say more? – and I felt sure his social status in Berlin, no matter how solid, would be considerably shaken if certain details of his *garçonnière* pursued him thither. Especially in such an unforgiving and puritanical climate.

And yet even this attempt proved fruitless. Well, I thought, nil desperandum. More irons! More fires! I sent off *Nuits Mauresques* again, this time to Paris (sooner or later the nettle would have to be grasped) and at once saw my symphony's ebullient Scherzo, too, might well stand alone. In fact, with its virtuoso brass writing in the Trio section it would do admirably as an orchestral *bonne-bouche*. Off it went, accordingly, entitled 'Entr'acte'.

I discovered I'd broken a lifetime's habit and was taking a sudden interest in the newspapers these days. I can now see that like everyone else I was gripped by the hypnotic approach of war which we all sensed in 1937. Since it is as easy to take up a newspaper for one thing as for another, I found myself turning from the politics of the front pages to things of lesser note. The second time I saw the name of René Martens (a piano concerto) was awful. The third time (a *Cantata Profana*) worse. His impertinent face even began to rise up and interpose itself between the peacock feather and the sky, eclipsing both. Wherever I looked his presence obtruded as a dark cast compounded of his face and my name, like a blot on the retina which floats over every scene. In exasperation I wrote to him once more.

Were we not both professionals? Surely there must be some sensible accommodation we could reach? This was a situation which could only harm us both . . . He never responded.

René Martens, René Martens, René Martens. Have you, my reader, ever repeated your own name to yourself until you were no longer sure what it meant? Or thought its ownership might as well be in other hands? I had Sayeeda steam his face off the wall and for a month I exercised brutally, *perdu*. I was crouching to spring so I built up my springing muscles in private, even as my manuscripts were finding their way like time bombs into the hands of some of Europe's most influential musicians: agents, conductors, fellow-composers. I had given this pretender more than enough warning. Yet one morning when I leaned my shaven skull against the wall, panting from an exacting set of flexions, I glanced up to see his face still there. Evidently my stupid peasant's steaming activity had somehow managed to transfer his image indelibly through the newsprint and on to the whitewash. Well, a few strokes of paint would soon deal with *that*, but for the moment there was work to do. I was even then finishing a fair copy of the symphony's first movement. It was, as I had discovered, imbued with a feverish sense of expectation, almost of anxiety. This, of course, was entirely deliberate and the following three movements had been expressly calculated to satisfy this unfulfilment, those hopes so exquisitely raised. It was hardly my fault that the idiots would be getting arousal without resolution. Off it went to Adrian Boult in London as 'Fantasy Overture: *Le Désir*'.

And now came news of fresh impertinences. A René Martens string quartet was premièred in Antwerp, my own natal city. A 'Jazz Concerto' (inevitably, and for the usual modish collection of saxophones, percussion, ondes martenot and banjos) was 'adored' in Copenhagen. Here I found a tiny crumb of comfort. The rocket had surely peaked and any moment now would descend, a feebly glowing stick. No serious composer would waste his time on those ham-fisted Negro syncopations in order to be fashionably 'in the swim'. But then after what was surely no time at all I read of the Paris première of his Second Symphony. Clearly, this was a vastly overblown affair – double orchestra, organ, double choir, everything but the kitchen sink – and had immediately become known by the title of Martens' own poem, of which the last movement was the setting: 'The Diaspora'.

Does there not come a time, my friends, when from beneath the successive hammer-blows of injustice a man may no longer complain of injustice? To cry injustice predicates redress; and there is no redress possible for the theft of time, theft of one's being. One day I was René Martens, lion-in-waiting, listener to an inner voice, attentive to every sound which life gave off. The next I was a nobody of the same name. One by one my teeth were pulled. Note by note the inner voice faded away, my

only companion, my love. On the table where once my
precious symphony had lain was nothing. A little dust.
Stains of ink. It had flown, fatally dismembered, in stout
yellow envelopes to all points in the musical world. And
not an envelope alighted in some grand and distant city but
the night before had seen one more triumphant concert in
another René Martens' career. Precisely thus had my own
last movement (which I had wanted to call 'The Sands of
Time' but which I'd consigned to the postal abyss as
'Introduction and Allegro for Orchestra') been overtaken,
eclipsed, ruined by his Second Symphony. No, this was
not mere injustice.

But if not injustice, what? Anyone living in my alley
would have known at once. Stupid old Sayeeda herself
would have come up with an immediate reply. 'Le
destin, m'sieur.' The Will of Allah. Karma. Kismet.
Crap. In my little private chamber on the outskirts of
nowhere I began to believe something far stranger. I
won't deny it took me many months to recover from my
symphony's death. Maybe I never really have, any more
than I have got over the waning of an inspiration which
once was so vivid and fertile. I would sit for hours,
listening and listening to hear if this stranger's attrition
had left me anything I could call my own and found it
hadn't. I could hear only the café, the tinsmiths; only the
children's squeals as they played among the pigeons, the
washing, the heaps of goat-fodder on nearby roofs. And
the muezzin, remorselessly hitting E♭ and sending up his

freshly minted platitudes punctually into the unheeding sky.

It was when I realised that René Martens had stolen my soul that the strangeness occurred and I began to look at him differently. To my initial disbelief I found myself taking the beginnings of an interest in his career. To say I rejoiced in his successes would be pitching it a little strong – then, at least – though by the time war broke out the idea of his distinction had a certain pleasurableness attaching to it. I can't put it better than that. Not a day went by on flashing wings, like the pigeons circling beyond my window, without my taking my usual walk at dusk (oh! those North African smells at dusk: dung fires, mint, olive oil, orange blossom, excrement), without my thinking of him, fondly almost, relieved nearly. For that was it. He had taken away from me a vast burden so that I could view his imaginary presence with something of the benign farewell one might bestow on a heavily laden caravan padding away as over a carpet spread towards sunset. Mauve distances. Somewhere else the hucksters and bazaars.

Everyone knows of his tragically early death, of course. Or rather, of his arrest and disappearance when the Germans occupied Paris. The exact circumstances will remain forever unclear but it is known he ignored his friends' urgings to flee to London or New York in order to finish rehearsing his Third Symphony. After that, who knows? An informer, a someone who wrote an anonymous letter? They were crazy and terrible times in which youth and promise – even genius, yes – were no protection. But no matter; his music is played today, which is what counts. Ever since the war my deafness has shut me off from that world entirely, but I gather that his Second Symphony, especially, is nowadays often played (I am writing in 1959.) The name René Martens is spoken of with pity, affection, reverence. In a sense I had always known it would be.

Records

THIS IS LESS a story than an account of Jonathan trying to blot out the sheer pleasure of being friends with David. Same school, same university; a shared flat in London while one became a civil servant and the other a barrister. Same tastes in music. Thousands of formative hours spent in each other's company. Maybe Jon and Dave are also Sandra and Kate (or Naomi and Ruth) – it's hard to tell from this side of the fathomless sexual divide. We must write about what we know.

What we know is that for years Jonathan and David seldom did anything of much importance without the other, and never from choice. From their first meeting at school their friendship had the quality of pulling others into its gravitational field so that their respective families, too, met and liked one another enough to pool their resources for joint holidays. It is probable that one summer in the Dordogne when they were sixteen David was smitten by Jonathan's sister Cathy and Jonathan equally taken by David's sister Fisty (short for Felicity). A month's sun-drenched chumminess fuelled by wine and

51

proximity no doubt provoked adolescent dreams that in due course each couple would marry and raise a family in neighbouring houses. And their children, too, would grow up inextricably close and intermarry, and so on for ever. Perhaps it was the girls who never properly intuited this romantic plan; two years later Jonathan and David could be found trekking together across Turkey with not a sister in sight.

'Anyway, from what I've heard the outback's not exactly designed for women's creature comforts,' Jonathan had said.

'Specially down towards Syria,' David agreed. 'If it's not Kurdish rebels it's Islamic diehards. They say only the toughest TV newshen survives. Still, I imagine we can do without girls for a couple of months if the rest of the experience is half as interesting as it's cracked up to be.'

'At a pinch.'

'At a pinch.'

They laughed. Had they been American college boys thirty years earlier they might have punched each other's biceps. Being British they contented themselves with an easygoing joke or two about being able to save on weight by taking only one pack of condoms. The holiday turned out a great success, an adventure, with enough shared hardship and alarms to make friendship feel like comradeship as well. The condom pack remained unopened, becoming flatter and more dishevelled the further it worked its way towards the bottom of David's rucksack.

There were plenty of distractions other than sex and besides, they were not in each other's company for more than twenty-three hours out of the twenty-four – sometimes less than that. They would split up for various chores. Jonathan would straighten up the tent and chip away at the frying pan while David practised his Turkish in the local village, buying lumps of salty cheese and lengths of fiery sausage. Now and then each would go for a judicious stroll while the other dozed or read or claimed to be finishing one of those increasingly crumpled letters which are never finally posted.

There were the usual disagreeable experiences involving stomach upsets, moonless nights, heavy rain and rags of wet newspaper. It was amazing, really, how intimate the pals could become while all the while preserving an almost clinical detachment, as when each inspected the other's pubic hair for crab lice which turned out to be Turkish fleas. Jonathan was particularly scrupulous on this occasion, slightly louder in his jocular protestations that only the duress of foreign travel could reduce him to the simian level of body searches. Slightly louder, too, were his exclamations of disgust one night five minutes after they had doused the light. They had been obliged for once to camp in an official site on the outskirts of a town and had pitched their tent on an allotted rectangle of bald soil. In the darkness Jonathan unearthed between their sleeping bags the cold, leaking, ant-covered remains of somebody's knotted condom. But then, of course, it was he who had to get up, wrap it in newspaper and wash his hands. It represented everything wrong with campsites and the two friends decided that in future they would stay in a town's worst hotel rather than endure such squalor. David never remarked on (and nor did his friend explain) why he should have been digging around with his fingernails in the dark between them. It was just one of those memorable episodes to be retold as a traveller's tale in a pub on their return.

The barrister-to-be and the future Foreign Office functionary came home tired at night, generally contrived to eat together and then spent most evenings in their own rooms studying the sort of large, dreary books whose mastery in youth implies the promise of a generous salary in middle age. But at weekends there were films to be seen, pubs to be visited, launderettes to be sat in and, well, girls to be chatted up. Sometimes the girls became involved in these ordinary pursuits. They were mostly fellow students on the boys' courses with well-bred faces and cars given them by their fathers. Jonathan's girls – if one could generalise from only two examples – had horsy tendencies and were good sports. They knew a lot about things such as Stockholm tar, wind-sucking and what to do when your Land Rover conks out in a snowdrift in the Mendips. His mode with them was that of a slightly younger brother, proud but a bit passive, as if hoping they might pass on their sensible lore. One day it would come in handy on the estate he was bound to have.

David's girls, by contrast, were frankly sexy; less handsome but clearly as knowing in the bedroom as Jonathan's were knowledgeable in the stables. Sounds of strenuous exercise would penetrate David's door and reverberate through the small flat while from Jonathan's room could be heard only the murmur of conversation, outbursts of laughter and soft classical music. Over Nescafé on Monday mornings David would rub his eyes and shake his tawny mane ruefully, the loose knot of his tie resting on his chest and his shirt collar still undone. 'These keep-fit classes of ours'll be the death of us,' he used to say as the early rush hour traffic sizzled slowly past in the streaming grey street outside. 'I couldn't hit you for a quid fifty, could I, Jon? I'm skint until I can get to Holborn and visit those apple-cheeked cottagers, Mr and Mrs Barclay plc . . . What a pal. Allow me to do the same for you at the start of the financial year.'

In order to reconstruct a rationale for what happened next one would probably have to presuppose some glum calculations on Jonathan's part. No guarantee they would be correct, of course, because we have no way of knowing how introspective he really was. What he did, in the middle of this matey domesticity, was abruptly announce his engagement to Van (Vanessa being the second of his large girls.) He stood one evening in David's room, his back to his friend, poking at a saucer of loose change on top of their landlady's atrocious marble mantelpiece. His face, reflected in the mirror hanging above it, was bemused, as if hearing his own words emerge was as much a shock to him as it was to David. Since it is anyone's guess, too, how analytical David was capable of being about such things, it may be fanciful to imagine that at that moment there flashed across his fledgling legal mind the image of somebody's being simultaneously defendant and judge; of entering a momentous plea while pronouncing his own sentence.

'Well,' he said in the fallen silence, 'I must admit you fair take a chap's breath away. Amazing news! Congratulations and all that. Golly, the whole route, eh? Bells, cakes, hand-held videos?'

'Hang on, Dave. I only said "engaged". It's that well-known statutory period. If the product fails to satisfy it can be returned and the cheque cancelled without loss of customer's rights.'

'That sounds like true love, all right.'

'Just realistic. Nobody ever said anything about renouncing one's intelligence in order to marry.'

'But it helps.'

Both were smiling now, collapsing back into the easy repartee of so many years. One of them put on a record of Mozart overtures. They watched some desultory television together, the cold glow making their faces a little older and more anxious.

'I don't suppose we'll ever actually get *married*,' said Jonathan at length. 'Van and me, I mean.'

Several glum days passed.

In the mind, famous for wanting total contradictions –
celibacy and a devoted marriage, total freedom and
absolute security, easy friendship and exacting intimacy –
the confusion is absolute. It is therefore impossible for us
(as for him) to decide whether Jonathan thought he loved
Van more than he loved David, or whether he even knew
that he loved David. What could three months have over
nearly ten years? Everything, of course, provided one
agreed with conventional notions of romantic love and
sexuality; provided you really believed that after several
weekends spread over sixty days you knew and were well
enough known to brave the next sixty years even before
you'd tried doing anything slightly stressful with your
new partner, such as sharing a tent on the plains of
Anatolia. Maybe Jonathan imagined that since sooner or
later David would announce his own engagement the
blow could be softened if he himself precipitated the
ending he most dreaded. On the other hand the reason
might have been that Van was quite a powerful gal who'd
decided that Jonny would do very nicely provided he was
treated with a firm hand.

Any of this, or none. All we can tell is from looking at
the friends' faces as they sat in front of their television, as
they chose a record, Klemperer versus Karajan, as they
came and went in the days following Jonathan's
announcement: a faint poutiness as if resenting some oaf
who had muscled in from nowhere and was managing to
turn one against the other by an illegitimate trick whose

effects neither could yet see how to annul. On the surface, of course, the badinage was as it always had been, though now studded with references to something never directly mentioned.

'With a feather is how you could have knocked me down, Jon me old lad.'

'You and me both.'

'Real grown-up stuff.'

'I know. Not too good, that part.'

'At least you'll still be a Bachelor of Arts.'

'Yes . . . Apropos of nearly nothing, Dave, how's old Fisty these days?'

'She's apparently selling futons in Banbury with this strange woman she's found. I'm beginning to suspect our Fisty may not be quite as other girls are. I know the mater thinks so.'

'Just as well we're not planning to marry, then. She and I, I mean.'

'I don't know what you did to the poor girl back in the Dordogne but I fear that's a non-starter these days.'

'I don't remember doing anything much.'

'Perhaps that was the trouble.'

'Bugger work. Let's go down The Castle and shoot some pool.'

The process, once blurted, wouldn't stop. It had its own inertia even as the friends laughed and joked and looked on helplessly. Van's family were no less determined than Van herself. One weekend Jonathan told her father in an elderly tone of voice that 'after due reflection' he thought the engagement ought to be longer rather than shorter because he wished to qualify first and at least have a salary on which they could live. Van's father, who had made a great fortune out of something or other, laughed and said how charmingly old-fashioned of him, that nowadays it was considered almost *de rigueur* for the woman to keep the man. 'All you have to do, Jon lad, is think of yourself as Van's permanent toyboy. Ask me, that's exactly what she needs.'

This light and depressingly accurate dismissal of Jonathan's most thoughtful delaying tactic made the whole thing inevitable. It wasn't that he didn't love Van. He did/believed he did/knew he would eventually. Like everyone else, he had grown up with the knowledge that sometime about now The Wife would appear and by some mystical process he would recognise her when she did. And the day had dawned and here she was and it turned out to be a bit like the doctor telling you out of the blue that he was going to have to take your leg off. Nothing a fit young fellow like him couldn't adjust to; it would mean a few changes to his lifestyle, of course, but it didn't do to slummock along indefinitely in the never-never world of student life. It might feel a bit strange at first but it would unquestionably be a broadening and deepening experience.

And as the young patient half believes all this is happening to somebody else, so Jonathan watched in paralysis as his casual declaration to a saucer of pennies took on the force of a promise, and his promise (which may or may not have been made with crossed fingers) hardened into an announcement in *The Times* of an impending wedding. All this while David was unable to help his closest friend. David, it was obvious, could never have been stampeded into marriage in such a fashion. He was far too planned, too considered. He would sow his oats until well after his exams, maybe until he took silk. He would have a lot of fun and then do the right thing by some girl he really liked and that would be that. He realised all was not well with Jonathan. He was also troubled by his suspicion that no matter how long he, David, knew her he would never warm to Van. There was a hard streak in her which was not so much determined as plain ruthless. Old Jon, by contrast, had a quality of gentleness you could spot a mile off. Sometimes people took it for weakness but anyone who had known Jon as long as he could recognise it as an endearing strength. Three months – well, four now – weren't anything like long enough for somebody of Van's steamroller delicacy to appreciate a person as complex and tenacious in his affections as old Jon.

But the longer things were left unsaid the less possible it became to say them, so that at last there remained little between the friends but their fond jocularity. At which point, of course, it is open to anyone to speculate that David's inability to head Jonathan off his course or even to

say 'Stop me if you think this is none of my damned
business but . . .' was because a knowing part of him
(about which he knew nothing) had already worked out
what the score was. It would only take a reasonable,
innocent question like 'But why *now*, Jon? That's what I
don't get. Why not in a couple of years' time?' to risk a
potentially traumatic outburst of truthfulness. Real
reasons. Hidden agendas. Cans of worms. Confessions.
And the confessions might be considerably worse than the
possibility (which had once occurred to David, affording
him a brief-lived reassurance) that canny old Jon was
marrying Van for her loot. But Jon, while having his wits
about him, wasn't canny in that sense. No, it was altogether
darker than that, and there were limits to what a chap
could be expected to deal with . . . Back at the level of old
pals David watched his old pal with glum concern. And in
due course he found himself robed in morning dress being
the best man, his cheery repartee sounding to his own ears
more like gallows humour as it tumbled efficiently out.

The episode which stuck most in David's mind had
occurred some weeks before, when the two friends had
been obliged to have a conversation about The Future –
specifically, what was to be done about the flat they were
jointly renting. Not even bluff humour could disguise the
unspoken sense of a marriage being brought to an abrupt
and unsatisfactory end in order that another might
abruptly and unsatisfactorily begin. Suddenly the mortar
of a shared life had to be raked out, exposing unwanted

joins of possession. Their extensive record collection, in particular, belonged to neither of them. It dated from their sixth-form days and had grown ever since. Hopeless trying to remember now who had bought what, though Jonathan had probably (had anyone been counting) contributed two-thirds. What mattered was their coincidence in taste, the long history of its broadening. With the brusqueness of atonement Jonathan on the spur of the moment told David the records were all his. For an awful moment David glimpsed tears in his friend's eyes which made it impossible to do anything but accept, even as he knew he didn't want them, not at such a price. Jonathan seemed no less upset that because of him David would be obliged to go through the vile process of searching for accommodation in mid-term, to move all these books from the shelves they'd put up, hide another landlady's lime-green candlewick bedspread, drop coins into a different gas meter, memorise a new phone number. At this sign of his friend's conscience David was obliged to turn away to conceal his own emotion, although that might have been pure self-pity: he was moving out because he knew nobody else with whom he could bear to share the flat.

Of course, both would have been vehement that a ten-year friendship would naturally survive marriage – proper friends were friends for life – even as both were filled with an apprehension that this was actually its end, here in this room of this flat on this particular rainy evening. Neither could think of a decent reason for any of it. The collapse and upset felt wholly unnecessary, yet that thought could never be spoken. It went equally unsaid that while no-one in his right mind relished spending Saturday afternoons watching his washing swirl and churn in a launderette's fungoid atmosphere, there would soon come a time when such amiable domestic rituals would be deeply missed. Pubs would seem emptier too, and games of pool become so rare as to be self-consciously nostalgic and hence not worth risking. By being suddenly rendered impossible, a version of the future which had hitherto remained properly vague now took on the weightiness of something denied.

So there it was. And at first it was David who was the harder hit since Jonathan was kept so busy with the new life Van's father was buying them, with generally making a go of things so he might safely feel his decision had, after all, been wise. On the surface David's own life went on pretty much as before, once he had installed himself off the Gloucester Road, except that he could never remember London weather being this dreary, life so unfunny and uncompanionable. His fellow law students were mostly useless at snappy one-liners. The girls he brought home did all the right things; but a weekend's passion lacked the sturdy resonance of ten years' companionship and Monday mornings were uncommonly hollow and grey. The record player remained perpetually silent. He and Jonathan rang each other up, of course, but something dense and opaque squatted on the line between them.

There was no casual way for either to say 'I miss you' without awful impropriety.

Eighteen months went by. There was a baby. Jonathan still looked too boyish to be a credible father. He had grown quite thin. From time to time David came to dinner and tried to practise the love that has no name. What could it be called, this commonplace, dutiful, genuine attempt to feel affection for your closest friend's spouse with whom one otherwise wouldn't care to spend five minutes? The love that grits its teeth, perhaps? This, David might have reflected, was maybe what Christians had in mind when they emphasised loving your neighbour despite a deep and instinctive dislike. And as in that case, one had to fall back on doing it for the sake of a third party. (It was still too early in his life to acknowledge that most of the people we wind up loving are *faute de mieux*, though it was not too early in Jonathan's.) For Jonathan's sake, then, David strenuously tried to love Van – so hard, indeed, that it never occurred to him to wonder if he were succeeding. Enough that she was old Jon's wife. Van, too, made valiant attempts not to write David off as a dubious hangover from Jonny's trivial, bachelor past.

Three more years went by; a second child. At last David, too, announced his engagement and asked Jonathan to be best man. Jonathan, by now quite gaunt, of course agreed. Like David before him he conducted himself with obligatory light-heartedness. He gave a little speech about having known Dave intimately for, golly,

it must be fifteen years now, it doesn't seem possible –
although the word 'intimately' should not of course be
misconstrued. (Laughter.) He looked at this elegant and
promising young barrister standing here in Moss Bros.'s
best and realised most people might have some difficulty
imagining him lying face down in mud dressed in nothing
but a tent. (More laughter.) He had been privileged to see
this by lightning's fitful gleam one stormy night in the
Turkish badlands. But he'd better let further details of this
– and even less repeatable – episodes remain decently
shrouded. About certain matters old friends' lips are
loyally sealed. (General mirth.)

A wedding guest, closely observing, might well have
beaten his breast on noticing how, from time to time,
Jonathan was casting the strangest look at David's bride,
shafts of purest haunt. Provided the guest wasn't too
drunk for greater accuracy he might have seen in these
looks the covetousness of someone who would have given
his very soul for the last few years to evaporate, to watch
the woman evaporate, to find himself standing there in her
place, booked for a honeymoon in Tobago. Certainly the
wedding guest might later have gone his way reduced to
pondering those endless imponderables about what made
people do the things they did, the unhappiness they
shouldered because they thought they ought to, the losses
unwittingly laid up on those boyhood plains of Anatolia.
By then, of course, the wedding guest would have been
pretty drunk. He might have beaten his breast with true

fervour had he also been able to see five years hence and know that Jonathan was to become a quite bad-tempered man, an easily irritated father who, each Christmas, sent a record token to his schoolfriend David for old times' sake.

Frank's Fate

I'D BEEN OUT of touch with Frank for many months when
his agent, Charlie Stedall, rang me one morning to tell me
he was dead. After the first downsinking shock a kind of
mellow merriment seized us both, as it so often does the
middle-aged on hearing the Reaper's tread pass close by
before it fades temporarily into the distance again.

'Well, poor old Bewley,' Charlie and I repeated to each
other in fondly reminiscent tones until he became an agent
once more and reminded me that I was Frank's literary
executor.

'So I am,' I said. I couldn't have forgotten but until that
moment I hadn't remembered. One of those duties
blithely undertaken years earlier when we were all young
and only old people died. The prospect was not cheering.
Frank Bewley had been famously drunk, famously careless, famously itinerant for most of his life. He had lately
settled in Italy and now had died there. My immediate
glum thought was that the undoubted chaos of his literary
estate would be compounded by undreamed-of complications in a foreign language. I foresaw having to deal with

Italian lawyers, publishers, bureaucrats – even, possibly, the very tax inspectors who had probably helped drive him to his early grave (he was forty-six). I'm not myself fond of travel.

'It'll be all right,' said Charlie unconvincingly. 'I'll try and come out at the end of the week to give you a hand. It might be an absolute riot. I don't see why old Frank in death should be any less colourful than he was alive. He'd have loved an opportunity like this. "Now *there*'s an article or two for the talented hack." '

His imitation of Frank's voice had the effect of saddening us both. Our friend was suddenly and irretrievably gone.

'How did he die?'

'Fell downstairs, apparently. Literally broke his neck, according to the British Consul in Florence, though he was only passing on what the police said. No dubious circumstances, amazingly enough. I suppose the poor old thing was pissed as usual. To be honest, I think you ought to leave at once. Today, if you possibly can. There's a complication. Gillian already knows.'

'Ah.' Gillian Bewley was Frank's elder sister, an unmarried lady of some fifty-five winters with not, to judge from her manner, a single summer among them. She was Frank's greatest champion. She knew he was a genius; disbelieved any version of her little brother which painted him dissolute; saw only conspiracy to deny him the various bays and laurels rightfully his. Gillian was not at all unlikeable, merely unlenient. One felt that from now on and for her benefit *nil nisi bonum* ought to be spoken of Frank's life and loves if humanly possible. It would be a tall order. Charlie Stedall had no need to explain to me how vastly preferable it would be if I could reach Frank's house before Gillian and remove the sort of things which might cruelly dent her image of him.

So I groaned, made lightning arrangements, flew to Pisa that same afternoon and – it turned out – had two days to myself before the grieving Gillian arrived. I did some hasty culling in Frank's library before pursuing my searches further afield, such as under the bed and in a galvanised steamer trunk. It was as well I did so. As far as Gillian was concerned her brother had simply been 'not the marrying kind' just as she herself was, and presumably full of her same fierce virtuousness. I, who considered I'd known Frank Bewley rather better than she, was quite prepared for what I found, even relieved that it was yielded up in such quantity. He seemed to have made few efforts at concealment and so, I reasoned, with any luck nothing too horrendous would surface later. The odd photograph dropping out of a book could always be explained away as having been left by a guest.

I soon sent up into a flawless Tuscan sky oily billows of burning rubber, film cassettes and glossy pictures, fuelled by quantities of amyl nitrite I had found in the fridge. While this awesome pyre of Frank's libido flared and spat and its smoke thinned to nothing towards the Apuan Alps,

I gathered up over two hundred bottles (there was even an empty half of Martell inside the grand piano) and dumped them out behind the garage. In doing so I nearly fell down the very flight of steep kitchen steps which had just done for Frank, and could now see it wasn't the ideal choice of house for a heavy drinker living on his own.

Only when all was clear could I settle down to my friend's literary relics. And here I was in for a surprise. I began to wonder whether any of us had actually known him as well as we liked to imagine, whether we hadn't too cheerfully connived at his own rueful self-description as a hopeless bohemian whose professional life partook of the same chaos as his private life – that the two were, in fact, inseparable. What I found, admittedly beneath a top-dressing of dust, fallen plaster and general litter, were fairly neat files of correspondence, labelled exercise books, manuscripts tied up with string. In short, an unexpected orderliness of a kind which looked to have been a habit rather than a recent access of zeal. I couldn't think how we'd none of us noticed.

I could soon see Charlie Stedall wasn't likely to make his fortune with a bonanza of posthumous Bewley master-pieces. As far as I could tell there was virtually nothing which hadn't already been published. Naturally enough most things – including the vast majority of the letters – tended to cluster around dear old Frank's one huge success, *Feathers*. In the current jargon *Feathers* had been a runaway bestseller and had made Frank (and Charlie too) a great deal of loot in its day, money which in Frank's case was long gone. It had been a book of its time, a heart-warming tale about a boy and an owl which – but I can't bear to go on. 'Absolutely nauseating,' Frank used to say of his famous story. 'Complete shlock. Though sadly I have to admit it's the shlock of a master shlockster.' If he revelled in the book's success it was only in the irony of it all. 'You've got to laugh. I sweat my guts out trying to write the litty stuffy I'd actually love to do and it vanishes without trace. Then in a kind of satirical rage I write the most ghastly story I can invent, somewhere between Richard Adams and Ernest Thompson Seton with a plagiaristic nod at *Kes*, and the thing takes off. The joke is, the bugger's been translated into more languages than there are literate nations. You don't suppose they know what a bloody barn owl is in Bangladesh, do you?'

I sat at Frank's desk and in the house's unbroken silence felt for the first time a melancholy shape itself around his absence. What a talented old thing he'd been! Behind the booze and debauchery and the ludicrous windfall of *Feathers* was a remarkable sensibility, some of whose manifestations I was unqualified to judge. In the piano stool I'd come on nineteen manuscript songs of his which I carefully tied up with the resolution that I would get someone serious to look at them. The piano writing seemed difficult. Approximately half were to his own lyrics. On the walls were a few of his watercolours – 'daubettes' as he used to dismiss them. I was fond enough

of one of his landscapes to make a mental note to ask
Gillian if I might keep it. Just that one picture; nothing
else.

Before she finally did arrive, tall and stately with woe,
I found in the bathroom a piece Frank had obviously
written recently. He used often to type out a first draft and
then correct it on the lavatory with a red felt-tip pen. It had
slipped down behind the cupboard which housed toilet
paper, mouse shit, and – thank God I looked – a half empty
bottle of grappa. I took it back to his desk and read it. It
was an essay, presumably designed for a magazine,
reflecting Frank's scholarly side and the one subject he ever
took seriously. 'What it all comes down to,' I could
remember him saying, 'is music. Old Pater was spot-on.
"All art constantly aspires to the condition of music," he
said, and so do I. If I thought I could compose a single
halfway decent bar I'd chuck this scribbling tomorrow. I'd
starve in a garret. I'd cheerfully swap *Feathers* for a fugue.
But I can't, that's the long and the short of it. All I can ever
do, in music or writing or daubing, is sodding pastiche.
Talent: five out of ten. Originality: zero out of ten. End of
term report.'

So I sat there in the silence and read what was surely my
late friend's last finished piece of work.

★

FRANK'S FATE
by
Frank Bewley

Writing from country to country we are inclined to feel a natural affinity for other journeyman artists who have always been led about by their noses, by their muses, by shifting patronage and chance. It is not always easy, though, to maintain that casual, workaday, drifting pose. To live and write in a foreign place, especially one which already has its polyglot artistic community, is to feel that community's unconscious sense of its own brilliance and, by extension, its conviction that anybody else coming to set up shop must be making some sort of claim about themselves. We intercept sharp sideways glances from those we know to be obsessed by questions of their own originality. Might we be stealing a march on them? (Do we care if we are? And we *are*.)

In my present home in Italy I sit in my isolated eyrie and gaze out across a seasonally sodden Tuscany. The woods on all sides are thick with maniacs in full paramilitary fig on wild boar search-and-destroy missions with rifles and dogs, their massed sweeps co-ordinated by walkie-talkie radios. Beyond this immense battlefield, among the hills and villages, lives the closely scattered foreign arts community. Serious artists all, keeping office hours and amassing *work*. It is all going on . . . While at night (so gossip runs) certain of the richer and more frivolous exiles gather and hold the most curious parties, really quite *louche*, some of them. Closer to my own house a penniless Hungarian concert pianist is trying to lay his hands on a decent piano.

The idea of a musician in a strange land urgently needing a piano, together with rumours of peculiar goings-on in shuttered villas behind high walls, suggests something I can't quite clarify: a nexus of knowledge which goes on skulking until one day a violent coincidence sets it free. I call on a friend who plays the viola; he wants to run through a sonata by Koczwara he has just acquired. We do so. Competent, unexceptionable eighteenth-century music; Haydnish in the early 1760s manner. I think little more of it until that same evening when I reach up to a high shelf for a book. It is not the Talmud and the entire bookcase does not topple over on me (as it did on poor Alkan, squashing dead Liszt's only real pianistic rival before he could even draw the moral). Instead, a copy of *Vathek* falls and hits me on top of the head to release in a flash that mewed-up bit of memory.

The year is 1791, a good fateful year for music. London – and to some extent England generally – is a veritable Tuscany of foreign artists. František Koczwara, or Francis Kotzwara as he has become, is only one of a floating population of Bohemian musicians. Another is Dussek, a far better composer and a friend of Mozart's currently living in Brompton. On New Year's Day Joseph Haydn lands at Dover on his first visit to England. Setting up amid the pastures of Lisson Grove, where huntsmen with their fowling pieces are to disturb his quiet, the celebrated composer casts about for a piano he can use. Dussek promptly lends him his in an act of true homage and friendship between exiles. Towards the end of May a great Handel commemorative festival is held over four days in Westminster Abbey. All musical London attends, including Dussek and Haydn, who is given a box of honour near the King's. Haydn has never yet heard any but bowdlerized Handel, a Handel cut or re-orchestrated to Viennese taste by Mozart and others. The sudden blaze of a thousand performers in the meaty English tradition, complete with trumpets *in altissimo* and great banks of wind instruments, knocks the old man sideways with its grandeur. When George III and the entire congregation surge to their feet for the Hallelujah Chorus, Haydn bursts into tears and exclaims, 'He is the master of us all.' This experience is destined to have a critical influence on his own late choral works, the six great Masses, *The Creation* and *The Seasons*.

Unaware that this is a seminal moment for a genius, and for European music in general, and somewhere among all those performers fiddling and blowing and singing their lungs out, are at least five of London's most raffish musicians. Haydn must already know one of them since she played at his benefit concert only a fortnight ago. This is Mme Krumpholz, the most celebrated harpist in town, whose reputation for virtuosity is in no way damaged by the public knowledge that her husband drowned himself in the Seine in the freezing February of the previous year – driven to it, they say, by her spectacular infidelities and tyrannous behaviour. Another participant is Francis Kotzwara himself, though it is not certain what he is playing since like Haydn he is a fair performer on every instrument in the orchestra. Kotzwara is by now forty or forty-one and a true vagabond. He probably arrived in England in the 1770s and thenceforth has shifted between London, Bath and Ireland, composing and playing and *getting by*.

At this moment in 1791 he is earning his daily bread playing the 'cello and double-bass at the King's Theatre in Haymarket. But Kotzwara has two additional sources of income. The first comes from an astonishing success he enjoyed three years earlier with his programmatic piano sonata *The Battle of Prague*. This piece became vastly popular practically overnight and is destined to run through upwards of forty editions in all sorts of arrangements in England, America and on the Continent. No doubt to his surprise after years of scantily rewarded hack-work (like the viola sonata I've just been playing), it becomes the most celebrated battle sonata of the entire eighteenth century and accords Kotzwara a *succès fou* if not *d'estime*, for in reality it is a truly dreadful piece of music whose worthless banality its composer must in his heart recognise since his other source of income depends on a highly sophisticated musical sense. For he is a professional pasticheur. He imitates the styles of his more famous contemporaries like Pleyel and Mozart and Haydn well enough to deceive even quite competent musicians and keep himself and several unscrupulous publishers in funds. It is strange to think of him playing away in the Abbey beneath the enraptured gaze of the great man whose style he often forges for a living.

By why did the copy of *Vathek* fall on my head with the force of a reminder? What has its author, that brilliant voluptuary William Beckford, to do with all this? Unlike tramps such as Kotzwara he was immoderately rich and privileged, having inherited a fortune when he was nine. He studied painting under Alexander Cozens and music under Mozart, if one may thus describe the odd lesson he received at the age of five from a nine-year-old Austrian wunderkind on his visit to London. The two met again briefly in Italy in 1770 and from then on Beckford enjoyed plenty of wanderings and exiles culminating in the scandal of the boy William Courtenay in 1784 which called for a judicious departure with his wife to Switzerland. In the meantime he had written his Gothic novel *Vathek*, whose inspiration had come partly from *The Arabian Nights* and partly from the infamous Christmas festivities held at Fonthill in 1781. This extraordinary occasion had involved the house being shuttered and sealed for three days' orgy, during which a Black Mass was celebrated. Among those present was a trio of Italian castrati:

Rauzzini, Tenducci and Pacchierotti. Rauzzini was director of concerts at Bath and thirteen years later Haydn was to stay at his house in Perrymead on his second visit to England and write the round 'Turk was a faithful dog and not a man' to Rauzzini's own words. Tenducci's style was little cramped by castration. He had already eloped famously with a fifteen-year-old girl and briefly fled England for debt. A friend of Mozart, who wrote him a *scena* (now lost), he was to marry three times and wind up in court for adultery. For his part, Pacchierotti was eventually to spend a month in prison in Padua for a political witticism and be championed by Rossini. All three had sung in *Il Tributo*, a cantata Rauzzini composed especially for Beckford's twenty-first birthday celebrations in September 1781. All of them knew Kotzwara, who was almost certainly at the notorious Christmas festivities three months later, revelling in the debauchery and marvelling at the cosmopolitan collection of geniuses and charlatans, lords and bawds.

Now, ten years later, who should be performing Handel in the Westminster Abbey jamboree besides Kotzwara? Why, Rauzzini and Pacchierotti (Tenducci had died in Italy the previous year). The three are amused to see each other with their shared memories of Somerset bucolics and much besides, and can doubtless spot among the thousand performers several others who have been party to various shenanigans at Fonthill and elsewhere. From time to time they catch the eye of another

Bohemian, Adalbert Gyrowetz, a young composer who in Vienna five years ago had had one of his symphonies performed and praised by Mozart himself. Now the impresario Salomon has just engaged him together with Haydn to write music for his Professional Concerts. Gyrowetz is currently writing an opera (*Semiramide*) in which Pacchierotti is to sing and in whose orchestra Kotzwara is to play . . . The shades of Handel hover and roll gloriously about the vaulting; the ranks of Court dress glitter and glow; the King is in his box, Haydn in his; God is quite conceivably in his heaven.

But as usual there is seediness and despair in the lives of those contributing to this radiant din. Unknown to all, poor Kotzwara is never going to play in *Semiramide*. He is about to become famous again. Not ordinarily famous, either, such as his *Battle of Prague* made him, but scandalous enough for Haydn to mention him censoriously in despatches and to cause a law court shorthand-writer's transcript of evidence to be torn up and burnt.

For, three months later on 2nd September, a Friday, he is making his way down Vine Street on the Strand side of Covent Garden. It is the lunch hour between one and two o'clock and it may be that he is already slightly drunk. It is probably not by accident he is walking this notorious area where the ground-floor front parlours of the houses are rented almost exclusively by prostitutes. From the doorway of No. 5 a woman accosts him and he hesitates. There is something in her voice or manner which attracts his attention for she is not beautiful nor even very young. Her name is Susannah Hill and she is twenty-nine. She was born at Frome in Somerset, not far from Bath; maybe it is her West Country accent which reminds Kotzwara of pleasurable times past. At any rate he goes inside and asks her if she would like a drink. She says she wouldn't mind a little porter. Kotzwara's own preference is for brandy and water and he gives her the money to buy both. At the last moment he adds two shillings for some ham and beef, for he is hungry.

When Susannah returns she and Kotzwara go into the back room where, having disposed of the brandy and meat, he makes ineffectual sexual advances. This may be a result of the drink but Susannah, who has seen all types come and go in her three years as a woman of the town, suspects a more fundamental problem. Her client's impotence distresses him; suddenly he offers her money if only she will cut his penis off. Horrified, she refuses. Kotzwara is deep in his gloomy fantasy, urging on her the knife stuck with grease and fibres of ham. When she still refuses, he agrees that he would be content to be hanged a little instead. Susannah protests that there's not an inch of rope in the house but this strange man with the foreign accent gives her some coins and tells her to go out and buy some at once, good and long. 'For,' he says, 'hanging I promise you will raise my passions.' Susannah walks the length of Vine Street but can find only two short pieces of rope which nevertheless seem to satisfy her client.

Kotzwara knots them together and makes a noose in one end which he slips around his own neck. The other end he passes over the parlour door and ties to the handle outside. In this way he need only go into a half crouch in order to bring about his own strangulation. Insisting that payment depends on her sticking to his demand to be hanged for five minutes, no more and no less, he at once bends his knees and the rope takes the strain. The whole operation has been carried out with a practised efficiency which reassures her that this is something of a habit with him. In any case she soon observes the effect he predicted. Maybe a strange delicacy or else her professional ministrations make it impossible for her to look up in time to see her client's blackening features. When after five minutes she cuts him down he falls heavily on his face and lies on the floor without moving.

Susannah's first thought is that he is having a fit. She frees the noose and runs over the road to her friend Elizabeth Dalton who lives in the house opposite. 'I have hanged a man! and I am afraid he is dead,' she cries. Together they go back. Kotzwara shows no sign of reviving. Leaving Elizabeth to do what she can, Susannah runs to the nearest tavern, whose publican is also a friend, and he in turn goes for a doctor who comes and unsuccessfully tries to bleed the corpse. Not long afterwards the terrified Susannah is arrested and taken to the watch-house in St Martin's. That evening she is interrogated and committed to the New Prison in Clerkenwell pending the Coroner's inquest. The next day she is charged with murder.

Kotzwara's death is the talk of London. The news-sheets are fascinated but details are lacking. Saturday's *St James's Chronicle* gives the fullest account while doing its best to accord the victim some sort of obituary:

> The name of the unfortunate man was Kotzwarra, a German; he lodged in Bentinck-Street, Soho; and was a Musician, and very eminent in his profession. He came from Ireland about a year since, being engaged by Sir J. Gallini for the Haymarket Opera-House, where he played the tenour the whole of the last season. From some very extraordinary circumstances, that came out upon the woman's examination, there is every reason to believe the man was insane.

Susannah Hill's case is heard a fortnight later on the 16th by Mr Justice Gould at the Old Bailey. The next day *The Times* reports the outcome with unavoidable self-restraint:

> *Susannah Hill* was put to the bar charged with the murder of FRANCIS KOTZWARA, a German, by hanging him at her lodgings in Vine-Street, St Martin's Lane: the circumstances of this case being extremely improper for publication, we shall merely inform our readers the jury returned a verdict of – *Not Guilty*. It appeared that the case could not be satisfactorily made out, and therefore the trial was stopped, after having engaged the attention of the Court nearly one hour. Indeed, it was the

particular request of the Court, that the notes taken by the shott[sic]-hand writers might be torn.

Eventually the buzz dies down. London's musical community stops missing one of its more dissolute characters; the waters of history close fairly without a ripple over Kotzwara's head while for the next fifty years his *Battle of Prague* sonata continues to outsell all Beethoven's. In any case this portentous year is still not out. Three months after Kotzwara, Mozart, too, is dead, a loss of which all Europe is conscious by Christmas. Still, the circumstances of the Bohemian's death are not easily forgotten. Luckily for us (the salacious, the ever-curious) the short-hand writers' destroyed notes were not the only source of detail. Someone in the Old Bailey that day must have had the sort of memory which stems from a vested interest. Shortly afterwards an anonymous book appears, written largely around the case. It is entitled *Modern Propensities or, An Essay on the Art of Strangling* and, although we learn little new about Kotzwara from it, we are given a good account of Susannah Hill, the country lass up from Somerset in search of her lover Thomas who had betrayed her and left her pregnant for the second time. 'The unfortunate Susannah sank among the vilest wretches,' the book observes, 'yet amidst this scene of riot and debauchery, she was visibly the most decent in appearance and language; no doubt, the result of a mind founded in a virtuous education.' That Susannah is in essence a Good

Girl forced into corruption is emphasised by a description of her in court at the point where she is allowed to step out of this temporary and horrid limelight and back into welcome obscurity. One hopes but doubts that she made it back to Frome.

> She was neatly dressed in common apparel; and, on her countenance we could discover nothing that seemed to indicate a rooted depravity; nor was there anything in her person particularly attractive: from which it may be inferred, that the unfortunate – if not lamented Kotswarra – trusted more to the *charms* of the *cord*, than to those of his *fair one*. When she first came into court, she appeared intimidated; but on her dismission, the signs of excessive joy were visible . . .

Poor Kotzwara! To have had the skill to pass music off as Haydn's or Mozart's at a time when Haydn was in town and Mozart still alive, yet to have been able to write nothing under his own name with heart in it or distinctiveness or which wasn't merely mellifluous eighteenth-century gesturing: this surely was a true impotence. It constitutes a corrosive knowledge such as haunts Jacks-of-all-trades. Playing in front of Haydn or holding Black Masses with friends of Mozart are as close as they may come to self-expression, even as they ply an honest profession as jobbing musicians.

This autumn two centuries later that notorious nonentity Kotzwara seems to haunt the house. I leaf through a bound volume I have had in my library for years: a

collection of late eighteenth-century English songs and
arias printed on the watermarked paper of the period.
Here are *scenas* from those operas by Rauzzini for his Bath
concerts; by Stephen Storace, his sister Nancy and
Michael Kelly (all friends of Mozart's); by Pleyel, Hook
and Shield, in any of whose orchestras Kotzwara might
well have played. At the front of the volume are two songs
billed as 'Mozart's Celebrated English Canzonetts'. Surely
Mozart never wrote such a thing? Haydn did; but Mozart?

Then for the first time I notice that on each of their title
pages someone has written in an ancient sepia hand the
letters F. K. For a long moment I wonder if I have before
me two of the ineffable Bohemian's bogus utterances.
Certainly each piece is Mozartean while neither is particularly inspired. After much foraging I finally identify them
as genuine Mozart: two obscure and minor works pirated
and set to unauthorised English words. One is a Masonic
song called '*Lied zur Gesellenreise*' (K.468), originally of
arcane and occult import and now blithely appearing as
'Henry's Fate' ('Hope alas! is fled from me, Henry's lost,
ah! lost at sea').

I am indeed sorry not to have a genuine Kotzwara
forgery in front of me, but I go on speculating all the same
while continuing to gaze out across our own community
of tramps. At the fag-end of a cultural tradition it appears
increasingly to matter whether one hacks a niche, no
matter how small, into the immemorial slopes of
Parnassus. This becomes still more true as suppressed

millennial frenzy grips us with the possibility that one day soon Parnassus itself may have to be bulldozed to afford a new view. The prospect is hideous, thrilling. In the meantime the scramble to be recognised by the only tradition apparently worth recognising is thought to transcend the mere earning of a living. Those glances one intercepts are full of dread. How can one infallibly tell charlatan from genius? Supposing it turns out that one of these local bohos living within earshot of the huntsmen's fusillades has been producing acknowledged masterpieces *and* going to all-night orgies? One supposes one must just go on working regardless (the glances imply), living as productively as one may in the undifferentiated shadows of genius and charlatan alike . . .

Only members of communities watch each other so nervously and think in such terms. The sole shadows in which I live are those of the usual mortal chills now hastening with fleeting blots of cloud across the October hills. A small sadness gathers – not for the pathologies and perversities to which anyone, including geniuses, may be prey, nor even quite for the pasticheur whose whole artistic life passes in perpetual strangulation by those he imitates. But the mere accident of playing a sonata and then having a book fall on one's head can be enough to jolt us momentarily out of that private patch of sunlight which we like to claim as our own unique creative space. Suddenly those wry internal clouds begin drifting across. Why are people so bothered about posterity? (how the proofs keep rolling off the presses!). W. T. Parke, in his *Musical Memoirs* of 1830, described Kotzwara as 'poor, although his talents were such that he might otherwise have acquired a respectable competency. In fact he was a genius, and like many of that class, as uncertain as the climate or the stock exchange.'

'Genius' has a different flavour nowadays. Our fellow exiles need not recognise it in the splendid, unscrupulous *getting by* of a minor character like Kotzwara now that he is safely and luridly dead. Their narrow glances are levelling, not elevating. Playing their game just for a moment, we indulgently suspect each other of being hardworking and unoriginal: small voices in no new mould, forging a living. Forging and re-forging that compulsive, private *pasticcio* like itinerant contract workers, like tinkers, plodding ever on with the backward lordly glance of mandarins.

ENDS

*

When I had finished reading, the late autumn light beyond Frank's study windows was already waning. Subdued, I went to his music shelves and looked up the pieces he had mentioned with their 'F. K.' intitials in faint brown ink. As he had written, there they were.

I flew back to London from Pisa taking few of Frank Bewley's literary effects with me. In the aircraft's hold were some folders of his letters and the original manuscript of *Feathers*. When Gillian had picked over the rest of his stuff it could be bundled up to follow in due course, together with the furniture and the grand piano. For now, I held on my lap what for me was his most evocative relic. I re-read it as we crossed Europe and was left in no doubt that when Charlie Stedall also read *Frank's Fate* he would think as I did. In his bleak and punctual manner and without for a moment foreseeing his own sudden death, our talented friend had contrived to write his own obituary.

The Dell

I WAS, of course, proud to be accompanying the Adeptus
into the mountains where he lived. Few pupils were
invited to spend time with him outside tuition hours, let
alone be singled out for a private journey. So my heart
was light as I hopped from shadow to shadow in his
thunderous wake, my new straw sandals singing on the
forest path like crickets at the season's height. My *tabori*
bounced in its bamboo sheath at my side, nestled in
crimson silk. From time to time I wondered where the
Adeptus had stowed his, for there was nothing tied around
his waist but his linen girdle. I presumed it was in the bag
slung over his shoulder, for how could a teacher teach
without his flute? Also, it was hard to imagine a man of his
legendary skill and fame travelling without his voice, so to
speak. As each variety of bird has its distinctive song by
which it can be recognised from one end of the country to
the other, so the Adeptus's *tabori* playing would be
identified anywhere and at once. Innkeepers would make
ready their best room; poets and even merchants would
sleep on the hearth with their dogs in order to say that the

Finch of Bado had passed a night in their own bed-chamber.

I was not a poet, nor a merchant, just a humble apprentice skipping along for happiness between the dapples on the path. Well, perhaps not altogether humble; didn't I just say I was proud? Humble about my own abilities, then, and proud that this famous Adeptus had chosen me out of all the Academy. Could I doubt that, no matter how short our time together, my playing would be transformed? I had already mastered all Thirteen Modes in Water, Sky, Mist and Rock. My rough passing was not up to much, admittedly, but would do at a pinch. Maybe the Adeptus was planning to start me on the Three Gateways as well as smooth passing? But no; that really was vanity on my part. Not even the most virtuosic musicians were introduced to such difficulties before they were eighteen.

'What did it say? What did it say?' broke in the voice ahead.

'Who, sir? What, sir?' I increased my skipping to catch up.

'The bell-bird.'

'Oh, Adeptus, I didn't hear it.'

'Did you even see it?'

'Not really, sir.'

'It had horns and was mooing. You missed a rare sight.'

A chastened silence was the best way to react to his more cryptic utterances. I listened out for a bell-bird but heard nothing but ordinary forest twitterings. The pine needles underfoot crunched agreeably. The early sunlight struck in golden shafts between the dark trunks. Every so often a large butterfly wobbled through a shaft on unmoving wings and for an instant blazed like a handful of flung jewels, to land on a dark bed of moss beyond as drab and unremarkable as a dead leaf. The sunward side of the rocks we passed glittered with mica and from time to time there were glimpses of snowy mountains so distant and so light their crenellations seemed to float halfway up the sky, clear blue above and misty blue beneath.

At midday we reached the Adeptus's house. At once I knew the stories about his austerity and simplicity were true. Less a house than a rude hut whose single room, floored with beaten earth, was only the size of six or seven mats. There was a heavy table with an inkstone and a few scrolls of music pinned to the brushwood walls with long thorns. A cape of oiled rhododendron leaves hung in one corner awaiting the autumn rains. Some rolled mats were tucked up into the rafters, together with a couple of soot-encrusted clay cooking pots.

'Should I call your servant, sir?'

'I have no servant, boy. You could shout till you were hoarse. Nobody would hear you but foxes and rock-doves.'

'Not even a boy?'

'No-one. If you would fetch some water from the stream I shall cook us rice.'

I couldn't easily relax as we ate. It didn't seem right that so great and noble a man should have cooked my food.

'And how was the stream, boy?' he asked while picking his teeth with a dried fishbone.

'Full, Adeptus. And as clear as glass.'

'But its sound?'

'Like rice wine flowing from the neck of a *chōsu* flask,' I hazarded, fidgeting a little. The image suggested itself in a flash; I felt something of the sort was expected of me, although truthfully I had never heard that particular sound in my life. I dared a glance at my master and was horrified to see his bushy gaze fixed on me accompanied by a sardonic rumpling of his scalp.

Without a word he got up from the floor, went outside and began blowing the cooking fire back to life. When it was sparking and snapping he sat down beside it and called me over.

'Sit,' he said, patting the ground. 'Give me your *tabori*.'

My heart leaped in anticipation. Already I was about to have a lesson on my own instrument. I unfastened the scabbard from my belt and handed it to him with a bow.

'Thank you,' he said and placed it on the fire.

Much, much later – months, in fact – I could acknowledge that moment as the beginning of all I have since become, albeit woundedly, like Goshō the village kid who was thrown by his horse and turned from being a dull boy into a brilliant cripple. I could hardly see for tears as the lacquer bubbled and peeled, the bamboo split and finally exposed my flute lying naked and innocent in its silk bed before that, too, danced orange and red and sank to char.

'I deserved that,' I said when I could speak, the obligatory phrase acid in my mouth just as there was acid in my heart.

Adeptus looked at me kindly and nodded.

'My father saved three years for that *tabori*,' I couldn't help adding. 'It was made by Nanjuk, the great craftsman.'

'Had it not been such a valuable instrument it wouldn't have been so valuable a lesson,' was the unyielding reply. 'Does one weep more for spilled water or spilled wine?'

'Neither,' I said. 'Only for a ruined instrument, sir.' It was an impertinent retort on my part and at once I steeled myself for more just deserts. But impertinence or not, the Adeptus seemed to have taken it to heart.

'We shall see,' he only said. 'And we shall hear. First we must hear. That was your first lesson, by the way.'

'The burning of my flute?'

'Certainly. Now we are equal since I, too, have no *tabori* here. I left all mine in my room at the Academy.'

I thought briefly of his instruments in their taffeta scabbards. All were priceless; the most famous was made from the wood of the very tree that had sung to the divine Shakoji the night before he charmed the unruly provinces into submission. Many said – and some certainly believed – that anyone other than an Adeptus who tried to play that dark and fearful thing would be turned into a lone pine tree standing by itself on the bleakest mountainside, waiting for the lightning bolt.

'It's time for your second lesson,' said Adeptus. He led the way to the stream where I had drawn water and followed it for some yards along a path which led among rocks and trees until we emerged on a promontory overlooking a series of valleys receding into misty distance. Here the stream spread into strands like a hank of horsehair dashed against the ground, each rivulet leaping and coursing its own way down among the boulders. The great teacher descended steeply. Seen from above, the brown egg of his skull gleamed among the rhododendrons, floating from outcrop to outcrop until we reached a place where the many rivulets became somewhat enclosed. On either side rose steep cheeks of rock bristly with plants and netted with vines. It was a dell of astonishing beauty, perched on the lip of space. Beyond, the wooded valleys fell off into deep forest which, tens of miles away, thinned into the emerald stain of fields. And floating on the far horizon were the mountains, the very margin of the world itself.

Here Adeptus halted and stood attentively, his head cocked. Then he busied himself at a pool little bigger than a rice pot which had been worn into the rock by a thread of clear water falling and falling on the same spot. He plunged in his hand and withdrew a pebble, paused a moment and withdrew a second one. Apparently satisfied, he moved to a rill which tumbled down a gully and tore away a dripping handful of green beard. I couldn't imagine what he was up to but he suddenly turned and motioned me over.

'Sit,' he said, pointing to a flat stone among ferns. 'Now tell me what you think.'

In some magical manner the stone's position seemed to be at the focal point of the entire scene. 'I think,' I said truthfully, 'I am surrounded by perfection.'

This was obviously inadequate.

'Everything tends to this point?' I offered timidly, remembering the famous quotation much repeated by our brushwork tutor.

'That could rightly be said about anywhere in the universe. I warn you, I won't put up with philosophy. I want detail.'

After a long pause in which I remained helplessly silent he said wearily: 'Close your eyes.'

Of course it's easy now to be surprised at my surprise, intolerant of my slowness. I would only say in my defence that I was infected by impatience. I was still upset by what felt like the wanton destruction of my treasured *tabori* and was vaguely expecting that Adeptus had brought me to this enchanted place as a demonstration of how contemplation of the beauties of nature could restore one's humility and bring one's petty turbulences to rest. It is indeed shameful for a musician to have to admit that until I shut my eyes I had heard nothing but the random sounds of water and pipits, my senses overwhelmed by the crude majesty of the view. But at once I was amazed by how loudly the waters sounded. Perhaps the dell itself acted like a conch, magnifying the slightest noise and focusing it precisely into the ear of the listener seated on that carefully positioned stone. The more I listened, the more I heard. The genius of the place had so arranged that each rivulet was clearly audible, with its own character, its own notes, so that one could concentrate on its individual song or, by an exercise of discriminatory control, blend it with those of its neighbours. The better one perceived how to play these games, the more arresting the effects. The slightest turning of one's head added further subtleties. Finally, all the voices could be heard together, still separate but concordant, individual yet harmonising.

'Oh master!' I cried in awe.

'It has taken me more than twenty years to arrange this place,' he said.

'You mean it isn't natural?'

'Of course it's natural, boy. I've simply taken the landscape and tuned it. Once upon a time the stream fell along its own bed near where you're sitting. Its sound was charming enough, to be sure, but unexceptional. With judicious damming and diverting I gradually obliged it to divide and subdivide again and again, each freshet following its own distinct course along a series of precisely graduated falls into cups and hollows of calculated size and depth. It was an act of will, just as hearing is itself an act of will. If you close your eyes again and listen you should be able to tell me how many streamlets there are.'

What a challenge for a musician's ear! It was useless trying to cheat and count them surreptitiously from beneath lowered lids since they were nearly all invisible from where I sat except as intermittent tufts and gushes scattered here and there among the rocks.

'Twelve, sir,' I said at last.

'Only twelve? Are you taking into account the one like frogs in a paddy?'

'Yes, sir.'

'And the one like crickets in a July dusk?'

'I think so, sir.'

'But not the wind-harp one? Like three swans flying south on a frosty morning?'

'Might there be thirteen, sir?' I concentrated still harder and then it suddenly struck me. 'The Thirteen Modes! That's it, isn't it? Yes, I can hear them now.'

'So,' said Adeptus, 'I was right. You're not altogether a worthless, baize-eared dunderhead. Nearly, but not quite. The Thirteen Modes it is. Nature is fine by itself but may always be improved by Art, you see. A boy such as yourself is a perfect example. I look upon you as a natural creature badly in want of tuning – or attuning, since it's only a matter of making you aware of abilities you already have. You should accustom yourself to sitting on that stone since I shall expect you to work daily in this place. Some of the time we shall work together but mostly you will be on your own. You think you already know the Thirteen Water Modes, don't you? I've no doubt you can play an approximate version of them on a *tabori*. But that's only an academic reading, the version one's taught with all

97

the right degrees of stoppling and quilling on appropriate notes. To be able to hear the Water Modes *as* water – ah, that's a very different matter.'

Was this, after all, the great secret of the Adeptus's miraculous playing, which by common consent exceeded that of any other flute-master as the mountain overlooks the dunghill? I had certainly never heard such a theory advanced in the Academy, where attention was always rigorously focused on the techniques as laid down by the old masters in the time of the Spice Kingdoms. But from the lessons I was privileged to receive over the next month I gathered the Adeptus believed the old masters themselves had derived their methods from the true Ancients, whose original practices had been lost or reduced to faint shadows by the discontinuities of time and warfare, of burnt libraries and civil unrest, of fashionable perversions and sheer indolence. He believed, in short, that the Ancients had long ago discovered the secret of tuning a garden or a landscape, that this secret had been lost, and that now by diligent research, meditation and inspired labour he had once more uncovered the source of our entire music.

The excitement of being the first witness to this extraordinary project – as he assured me I was – helped make up for the loss of my flute. I still missed the conforting tap of its sheath at my thigh, the feel of its length in my fingers, the familiar bristling of its quills and stopples, but I was willing to submit to my master's knowledge and experience. If I would be better off without a *tabori* for some weeks, then so be it. Each day at dawn I sat in the dell and listened for two hours without moving. Then I went and described my work to the Adeptus who would make excellent suggestions for achieving greater discrimination, for preventing other sounds such as birdsong from being a distraction, for maintaining a light alertness without fatigue. After this I would go into the forest and chop wood for the cooking fire, gather berries and fungi, dig for tubers, set snares and lime for the abundant small game. Boiled bell-bird became, I'm glad to say, something of a dietary staple for us. As far as I was concerned the species was well served for having been instrumental in my humiliation on the way up. Apart from cold mists at dawn and dusk which came ravelling through the trees like shawls the weather was fine, a noteworthy matter less for reasons of our comfort than because rain would surely affect the dell.

The Adeptus confirmed this. 'You may have noticed the earthworks upstream? In the case of a heavy shower I can more or less divert excessive flow; but winter rains and the spring melt produce torrents which swamp every-thing. It's a great task for early summer to restore everything to its place. It takes many days to remove the rubbish and re-establish exactly the former channels, uncover the chords and intervals. It's a very pleasurable job and one I look forward to in the sad days of winter. I did once try to build a series of ice chimes to wile away the

hoar season but they weren't very successful. It's a source
of great contentment just going from one little pool to
another, adding a stone here, removing one there, taking a
dead twig from a channel where it juts over the edge and
forms a false spout. All these things can instantly be
heard.'

Since I'm in part writing this as a memorial to him, the
greatest musician of the modern age, to the Finch of Bado
himself, I ought to set down those of his sayings which
fixed themselves in my retentive, if wilful and boyish,
mind. I deplore absolutely the increasing sentimentalisa-
tion of his life and achievements, suspiciously undis-
couraged by those jackanapes at the Ministry of
Pilgrimage who stand to benefit from the ever-swelling
hordes tramping up and down a once-lovely mountain
path to his once-simple hut. To refer to him semi-
officially as 'The Sublime Linnet' is frankly vulgar; while
the stubborn refusal to restore his dell to its former
auditory glory is little short of a national scandal and
should redound to the Academy's eternal discredit. This
cult of my Adeptus as a 'personality' obscures – as is no
doubt the intention – the radical element in his thinking.

'It is better to remain wordless, but not necessarily
silent,' I remember him saying one day in answer to a
naive question of mine about the relation between Nature
and Music. 'We have the gift of comment but we should
play our remarks. When the cuckoo calls from the wood
or the bell-bird chimes to the morning sun we should

never mimic them. That would be a gross disrespect. The idea of trying faithfully to imitate a particular bird or animal is anyway crude, let alone the sounds we might make. We musicians should leave that to the huntsmen. As we don't understand what they are saying it would be like trying to talk with an outlander by mindlessly repeating his every phrase. That would soon lead to blows because mimicry always has a satirical streak.

'When a Zen master give a *koan* the proper response must be immediate, unthought, its validity often being all the greater the less appropriate it seems. The master will know at once if his pupil is faking by using intellect to furnish authentic-sounding gibberish. Now this is the same gift which the true *tabori* player has: that if his understanding is genuine he can make the cuckoo and the bell-bird listen to *him*. They won't listen to stringed instruments, no matter how well they're played. Remember the story of fat Gokin and his lyre: the herd-boy who sat and played while the birds and fieldmice crept up to listen? And how his rival in love, the envious and sharp-witted Apat, pointed out that they only crept up during lunch, being dead to his playing but fascinated by his crumbs? Lyrists pluck and strum in vain and the most accomplished drummers, too, are wasting their time if they want Nature's attention. But a *tabori* master has the ear of all creation.'

On another occasion he said:

'In this matter I firmly believe the Ancients were right:

that it is useless to teach anyone to play an instrument until first they have been taught how to hear. For years an apprentice tea master never touches a teapot. Instead he is trained to discriminate. He learns to identify four hundred teas by smell alone. He learns to tell the taste of water made from November snow from that of February snow; to judge between roof snow and mountain snow; between this well and that well, one spring and another. All this until his palate has the required sensitivity and it is worth teaching him the actual brewing of tea. Your true musician is the same. He should refine his ear before he even picks up an instrument. Anyone can learn technique and anyone can be taught to play with the simulacrum of musicianship. But it is the ear and not the fingers which finally identifies the true master. This was the Ancients' great lesson to us. And this' (he indicated the tuned dell) 'its proof.'

And on still another:

'You have learned to hear the thirteen streamlets as thirteen streamlets or as one. Now you must hear yourself in them. Where is your own heartbeat in all this? Does it knock in your chest, or tick in your throat, or hum in your ears? It's there somewhere. Listen for it, then give it its place in the general panorama. Without the constant awareness of your heart your breathing will be wayward; and wayward breathing contravenes the second of the Eight Disciplines.'

'Ah, the Eight Disciplines!' I said to myself satirically,

for I was in my own springtime and found it hard to sit for hours just listening to streams or even to pay sufficient attention to the Adeptus as he spoke. Today this will sound outrageous, a typically impious confession. Yet it was so; and it was an early symptom of the most painful part of my story.

After a month the Adeptus decided he would return for a while to the Academy but that I should stay behind and improve my listening. So that I shouldn't be lonely and become depressed up in the forest on my own he said he would immediately arrange for someone to fetch me up a fresh sack of rice. Then, he said, when he himself returned he would bring me a *tabori*. The day after he had left a figure appeared on the track stumbling beneath a heavy load. It was – and this is where the Adeptus showed his understanding – a deaf-and-dumb girl from the town with muscles far stronger than her fourteen years would warrant. Her condition precluded idle chatter, which was no doubt the idea behind her choice, while her taking over the cooking and foraging released more of my time for self-improvement. That, too, was no doubt the idea, although it didn't quite work out to plan. I spent far too much time learning from her certain other fine discriminations which the Adeptus – genius though he was – would have been as incapable of teaching as I should have been loath to learn from him. Nevertheless, in a mere three weeks I could honestly claim that every one of my senses was much improved.

But all this while, doubts were massing in my mind in a way which was to lead eventually to great sadness. On the day before he had left I asked the Adeptus what it would sound like to play on the *tabori* the songs the peasants sang. He had looked at me in genuine bewilderment. 'But they could easily be played,' I persisted, 'simple tunes that they are.'

'Inconceivable,' he replied when he could speak.

'But it *could* be done,' I persisted in my temerity. 'Just as a cantonal potentiary *could* marry a prostitute.'

'Hush, boy!' he rebuked me, casting a glance around us at the unheeding forest. 'Watch your mouth! Some might construe that as satire, and the tongue-puller has often been summoned for less.'

That was, as a matter of fact, my first political joke, since just such a man had recently married just such a woman in a neighbouring canton. Still, the point had been made. Peasant songs were for harsh, drunken voices and one-stringed fiddles in taverns: they would have defiled the noble *tabori*. Even the thought ought not to have been thought; and yet it had been, and it stalwartly refused to un-think itself. During the Adeptus's absence I had pondered this and other related matters which, when he had duly returned, would surely have to be aired.

Yet when he did come back he brought me one of his own treasured *tabori*s which he presented to me formally, together with a scabbard and a mother-of-pearl box containing spare magpie quills and springs of bear's bristle. I knelt before him, overwhelmed by fondness and gratitude.

'Get up, boy,' he said. 'You can't play on your knees. Give me a scale of the Ninth in Water.'

Oh, to hold such an instrument in my hands! I checked the quilling, blew gently down the helical bore to warm it, played the scale.

'And now try the Third in Mist.'

I did; and all humility apart, it sounded to me as though I had much improved, and all without touching a *tabori* in over two months.

'Seventh in Air.'

Soon I was playing texts instead of scales. I managed 'Cranes in Flight' and 'Catching the Ox' but the 'Wagtail's Lament' defeated me. At which point the Adeptus produced another instrument and took the music up from where I had left off and I could feel the gooseflesh rise on my arms and neck, such was its beauty. How did he achieve that abstracted melancholy, the leaves' fall, the shiver of wind on the water's face, and all without losing the wagtail's lonely song? But after all, wasn't this exactly what I was here to learn?

Not altogether. And even after all these years it still grieves me to remember how powerfully that foul dissent rose in me.

'Who gave us the Seven Hundred Texts, sir?' I asked one evening after his return.

'The Ancients, of course.'

'Are you sure, Adeptus? Is it certain that it wasn't the old masters?'

'Where tradition is concerned, questions of certainty don't apply.'

'But the Texts had to come from somewhere,' I insisted. 'There must have been an occasion when they were played for the first time.'

'No doubt. That's only reasonable. There are musicologists who study such things. We're musicians. It's enough that we play the Texts as they have been perfected.'

'Supposing,' I began, and I could hear the nightbound forest surrounding the hut hold its breath, 'supposing one wanted to invent a text of one's own?'

For a long moment I could feel my master's eyes on me across the dying fire. 'And are these the sort of thoughts you've been having up here in my absence?' he asked sadly. 'I send you the comfort of peasants and you begin to think like one? Once you asked me about playing folk ditties on a sacred instrument and now you wonder if you mightn't invent *tunes*?'

'Not tunes, sir. Proper texts.'

'Improper texts, you mean. There are seven hundred Texts, no more, no less. They comprise all music, as bequeathed us by Nature and the Ancients. There is no other. All else is trivia and heresy.'

In cold print, I suppose, my part in this conversation reads like the triumphal rebellion of youth. In fact it was causing me nothing but pain. Uppermost in my mind was the sense of my own treason. Was this the way to express joy and gratitude to my Adeptus for giving me his marvellous instrument? Did it show me as worthy to share his laboriously rediscovered secret of tuned landscapes? Yet the irony was that the magic dell had itself inspired these thoughts, setting them free like geese which hear their companions calling in the mist and know it is time to migrate. There was nothing for it but to fly on; there could be no turning back. With a heavy heart I asked:

'Why is it, sir, that there shouldn't be fourteen modes? Or forty? Or four hundred, even? Why just the Thirteen?'

'That's like asking why there shouldn't be thirteen months in the year instead of just the twelve. The moon's periods are ordained by Nature. So are the Thirteen Modes.'

It was a useless, sterile conversation and we soon lapsed into an unhappy silence which lasted three days. I sat in the dell for hours at a stretch as a kind of penance so that Adeptus would recognise my submission. As soon as I did the peaceful sunlight, the stipple of the pipits' song and the artfully contrived rills all conspired to fill me with a sense of its completeness. Why look further and imagine vanities? Here I could safely gather about me the boundlessly subtle cloaks of the Ancients, of my own Adeptus. I could be secure beneath his aegis and in due time be virtually guaranteed an enviable post as a Court musician or as a cantonal lord's musical attendant. Was I ready to throw all this away, besides causing my master the unhappiness and offence I could already read in his face?

The answer must have been yes, evidently, for that is the way history turned out, with my entire life a political joke. How am I to express my utter grief for all that happened, yet without a trace of remorse? For instead of returning to the Academy I headed on over the mountains to a life of penury and notoriety. Since my music is officially banned I shall never hear it performed in the country of my birth, which is a sad matter to me. But of course that private regret is insignificant beside the great earthquake, whose twenty-third anniversary is today, which destroyed so much more than my own chances of making amends to a man I loved and revered. Not long after I took my leave of him the Adeptus was crushed beneath a boulder as he was seated on the very stone where I had sat long hours. He was only the most illustrious casualty out of many thousands sustained in the region, including those caught beneath the Academy's collapse.

Oh, that so much might be brought back! The Academy, naturally, resurrected itself in a jiffy but the Adeptus's priceless *tabori* collection within was smashed beyond saving. The man himself lay for two weeks beneath the boulder on the mountainside before his body was discovered by searching students many days after foxes and ravens had made the same discovery. No-one had known of the dell's existence, which is why they took so long to find it; and once having found it they couldn't recognise it for what it was. In their defence it must be said that the earthquake had ruined the stream's course, displacing aquifers, blocking off springs and opening new channels everywhere so that the escaping waters had resumed their course in the old bed. Needless to say, the dell has never been acknowledged as a musical instrument and now probably never will be. I – who might have learned from my master the exact techniques for tuning a landscape – I never did, and am now a pariah and a renegade and no-one would listen if I told them of the Adeptus's discovery any more than they would if I said it was high time to close down the Academy, for students and teachers alike to lay aside their instruments, abandon their finger exercises and spend a long sabbatical listening most carefully to water. No, it is so much easier for them to become virtuosos.

My last grief is most nearly that of son for father, which makes it the more intense. The Adeptus taught me everything I am; but he wouldn't recognise what I have become. He was indeed like a father to me; yet he would surely deny his offspring. I owe him everything; he would refuse the debt. Can anything be sadder than this? That he would consider my love had turned into betrayal when I am daily discovering the importance of all he taught me? Away beyond the mountains I make my own wilful sounds which he would never have accepted as music. 'What are these strange effects, these monstrous wailings like the winter wind, going nowhere and doing nothing but spreading a chill?' I can imagine him saying. But I only make them because years ago I heard something he himself never heard, something subversive in what the water said. It's there and he missed it. Underneath, though, there's truth in what he knew: that people hear but they don't know how to listen, just as they can speak yet can't bear to remain silent.

Knight

THE BOY had never understood why they hadn't taken the Major north of the DMZ to the Hanoi Hilton or whatever place of long-term imprisonment. Surely it would have been easier than lugging him along like unopened baggage whose contents – if ever they could be disclosed – would now hardly justify his dead weight? He had watched the Major trying to adapt to each phase of the new life which had begun the moment he stopped falling from the sky. A month of improvised tiger cages would be followed by shapeless weeks of forced marches along mountain trails. After that might come a period of comparative ease bivouacked on a steep forest floor, tethered like a goat to a tree. He was familiar with dead sticks for legs after being made to crouch all night; with blindfolds; with tied hands. Foreign words hurtled at him and past him until this world into which he had descended blurred beyond being a succession of places into a waste of pain and apprehension.

The Major was stubborn. He had known what to expect and for the first month had clung mentally to the place he had abruptly left, the floating city within sight of the coast where he had been an aristocrat, a knight steeped in knightly codes and valour. Ham and eggs, toast and jelly were still undigested in his stomach as he dropped like a helpless god into a land of rice and rotted fish sauce. He had fallen into a paddy, embedded to the hips and taken easily by what seemed to be chattering children in straw hats. At the very moment when his F4's arrestor hook ought to have been snagging the cable, allowing him to climb down (triumphant gladiator) to the rubber-streaked deck and go below for debriefing and real brewed coffee, the Major was lying trussed and slimy in a hut. Outside, the selfsame morning wore on. Only the universe was changed in a discontinuity so shocking as to seem part of a dream. Just as an infantryman watched in his mind's eye a comrade treading on a mine, so a pilot envisaged only other pilots being shot down. Imagination was a movie whose principal actor arranged for disaster to strike a limitless cast of shadowy stand-ins while he sat in the stalls chewing popcorn. When this rule was violently over-turned and he found himself rudely dumped through the screen up to his waist in pigshit his mind couldn't take it in. He sought refuge in his training. The interrogations began and he gave only the information which could be read on his dog-tags, sometimes whispered, often screamed. He lost consciousness with his own name on his lips and revived to hear his mouth chanting his rank and number.

The boy had first appeared the evening they invaded the

Major's body with a piece of bamboo. It was a lengthy session, designed to break him rather than to elicit military secrets. Those humiliations had dragged on for weeks until infection set in, then fever, and in his emaciated state they had to give him doses of antibiotics looted from US medical supplies. The boy stood outside and watched the Major leave his body and take up residence in him. Together they observed the knight gyrate and yell and not break. And all the while, they could see, there was a single humiliation he feared still more, which was the sight of himself filmed in harsh studio lighting, confessing his guilt and denouncing his countrymen. The Major had seen such films. The captives were docile, unrecognisable, speaking in unmodulated voices as they read out prepared confessions which always began 'My name is — and I am making this statement of my own free will.'

No military secrets, then, because he knew none to divulge, other than ephemeral ones of shifting tactics and the radio codes of a week long past. But secrets of a different kind were dislodged by the battering of his personality. The knight went on calling out his name and number even as he lost all sense of what the words meant or to whom they referred. Elsewhere within, lumps of this gallant construct, the fighting man, fell off to reveal the child he had been (timid of his father, quick to cry, idolising his piano teacher when his classmates were full of their baseball heroes. Never effeminate, merely radically gentle). And then the long haul of adolescence when he had put together this workable trick of concealment. He had become more competitive than his fellows; had dated the prettiest girls and driven the hottest cars over the old moonshine roads of his native Virginia. He had missed Korea by miles but flew himself up through the ranks while his father, the frustrated cold war warrior, finally glowed and proudly shook his red wattles. He had nearly piloted the U-2 in which Gary Powers was shot down in 1960, having been posted to Europe and the shrouded world of reconnaissance. From a succession of air bases ringing the Iron Curtain he had flown bloodless high-altitude missions for a short while. Back in New Mexico he had tested blind landing systems, had hardened into a husband and moved into married quarters. He was thought too quiet. People were suspicious of privacy even as they defended it as an inalienable right. He was not unpopular, but neither was he greatly loved. His artful student gregariousness had long worn off. Colleagues obscurely felt his remoteness might actually be disdain, but since he was an exceptionally fine pilot they ascribed it to dedication: that and the tense, lonely hours spent eighteen miles above the lunar landscape of Kazakhstan or wherever, expecting a heat-seeking missile. Still, his wife Cathy was a college graduate. How many pilots in 1964 married experts in French literature? Not that she gave herself airs and graces. Just that you couldn't help noticing if you dropped in that there were shelves of books everywhere and string quartets and stuff playing quietly. Unusual, anyway.

So in a sense the possibility of being shot down had been on the agenda for some years. That it finally happened in Indochina instead of somewhere in the USSR was a mere detail. For too long he had been a man out of place, straying far over territory whose inhabitants believed fervently he had no business there but whose anger was held at bay on the far side of a fail-safe screen of technology. Now it had failed, and he wasn't safe at all, though the fact that he hadn't yet been killed did suggest he was of value to someone. It was probably lucky that the Vietcong cadres through whose hands he had passed in the first few days had been in close contact with an NVA unit. Well-trained professional officers had taken him over from the peasant guerrillas and had marched him away along the endless trails which led to wherever he now was. Gaunt, feverish and tottering, he had been inherited by one unit after another, as far as he could judge, all the while getting no nearer to a proper camp for prisoners-of-war or to that dreaded studio in Hanoi where drugs, emotional blackmail or more terrible inducements might lead to him pressing the chicken switch on film, for all the world to see and despise, for his father to watch.

But where was he? The Major thought he had probably walked the Ho Chi Minh trail in all its tributaries and in every direction, starting westward over the hills into Cambodia. 'Walked'; but there was no real word to cover being dragged at the end of a rope while wearing a wooden yoke, being prodded with bayonets into a shambling trot,

being rolled down a thorn-tangled slope into a clear
stream amid laughter. And then unexpectedly finding
himself being strolled in a comradely way along a trail one
beautiful morning. When had that been? Months ago.
Like being reborn. The early sun dappling the clearings
through which they passed; the generous bowl of rice
gruel for breakfast; the scent of freshly lit Marlboro
cigarettes (how did an NVA field unit far from home get
those?); the young captain who spoke French and English
chatting beside him like a campus friend. A brief inter-
mission, that. All part of the softening-up process, he
thought. But 'walked'? No, you had to invent a new verb,
something like 'forced-wandered'. Resisting (only just)
the blandishments of company, the Major still clung to his
old formula: name, rank, number. Inwardly he felt a pang
like a lover's on learning that the friendly captain had been
posted away.

But where was he? The strength of human intelligence
is that it can dwell in the imagination while also taking an
acute interest in its physical surroundings. The Major
clung to the thought of seeing Cathy again, but in other
respects he had switched worlds. Now it was the aircraft
carrier and his former life which hovered like something
dreamt, something once seen on television. He had even
switched sides – or, at least, the whole issue of side-taking
seemed an invention. For much of the time, day and night,
month after month, his forced wanderings had been
accompanied by explosions, often beyond the horizon but

sometimes frighteningly close. These were the bombs dropped by B-52s out of Thailand, Guam, who knew where, up and down the Trail. Countless tons of high explosive falling from airplanes so high they could neither be seen nor heard. H & I. Everywhere were enormous craters full of stagnant water, patches of forest reduced to matchwood, in one place a river casually re-routed by a collapsed ravine. Harassment and Interdiction; and it was the Major who was being harassed. In combat 'friendly fire' might describe a tragic mistake, malfunctioning equipment, incorrect orders, blind panic and even revenge. But this was not a combat zone in the usual sense. Half the time it wasn't even Vietnamese territory. Bombs simply rained endlessly down into a rural backwater where they harassed and interdicted duck farmers, monkeys, virgin forest, conscript children pushing bicycles laden with howitzer parts or medical supplies, downed US Air Force majors. The issue of side-taking became blurred as he and his captors alike hugged the ground and was made no clearer afterwards when confronting the effects, ears still singing. Strangely, on the rare occasions when the bombs hit people the survivors never rounded on him in vengeance. It was as if to have lived through it was enough to be going on with; as if also his own bleeding and muddied body showed which side he was really on. The Major, like most airmen, had never witnessed ground combat first-hand. All he knew of war's cost was, by chance, what he was now seeing: mainly

peasants and boys in uniform doggedly rebuilding huts
and bridges and replanting ricefields and carrying on.
Some vast Gulliver had chanced to lie down on their world
and they were either stealthily pegging him down, strand
by imperceptible strand, or else they knew it was only a
matter of time before he rolled over in another direction
and they would be free again, like crushed grass crinking
itself upright. For the moment, though, Gulliver was
everything and everywhere, in the form of looted 'C'
rations, Marlboros, field dressings, ponchos, even the
woks and saucepans beaten out of the airframes of crashed
American planes.

So the Major moved nowhere, month after month,
covering great distances in great pain, losing sides.

He was taking it a day at a time, sometimes still capable of
admiring a dawn and often amazed to see another dusk.
He was certainly able to reflect (he told the boy) that it had
been a close call with the young captain. His entire life had
been wrenched apart and restructured, a highly emotional
business: he longed for an alliance with another human
being. A fatal weakness, of course. They'd sniffed that out
and no doubt ordered the captain to befriend him, to
saunter alongside his hobble to talk about *Le Grand
Meaulnes*, or why Edward Lear had painted better parrots
than Audubon, offering him Marlboros, avoiding all
mention of politics except to make a few risky quasi-
nationalist remarks about how many centuries of enmity

lay between the Vietnamese and the Chinese. This, the Major had guessed, was calculated to make him lower his guard. Were they not both of them educated and sophisticated men who knew that the emptiness of Communist rhetoric about a thousand years of friendship was simply the counterpart of White House blarney about impending victory? What survived, of course, was culture of a deeper sort, an observant human irony which transcended the idiocies of local dialectics. Men of the world, in short, finding that world savage and opaque and hoping to establish a small island of mutual sanity . . . And how nearly the Major had been suckered into yielding! The beautiful French, the touchingly flawed British English (where had the young captain learned that?), a comprehensible language at last in which – had he not caught himself in time – he might have begun to express himself in other than parrot fashion.

Yet without knowing it the Major had failed. He had not asked himself why they had tried this tactic. Why hadn't the captain talked about baseball or A. J. Foyt's chances of winning the Indy 500? Why hadn't he chatted about Zappa or Jagger or Diana Ross? How much, in short, did they already know about him? But stupefied as he was by his pains and loss, it never occurred to him that he might not be as anonymous in his rural backwater as it was to him. He tried talking to Cathy, but she skidded into the young Vietnamese captain, jaunty with bleak quotations from Baudelaire. She was too far away. He could feel her rendered vague by distance, thinning and wavering. The boy he had been, though, was made of more enduring stuff, surviving his father's anger as he now was managing to survive, day by endless day, the general fury ranged against him. Inflexible as ever with his captors, he had moved inside himself, going backwards. 'Of course,' the boy told him reasonably, 'it wouldn't matter any longer if you did make a bogus confession. Nobody would believe it. Nobody in the States would believe it any more than the Vietnamese themselves. It would just be an exercise in pure rhetoric. Only you would believe in it, in fact. We've seen the real war now, right? We've seen what's really happening on the ground, how little it has to do with issues of ideology and principle and everything to do with atrocious error, with expediency and face-saving. And we genuinely *are* sorry, aren't we? Contrite and ashamed to be part of something so lethal and catastrophic, breaking open the lives of distant innocents who did nothing to deserve it. Not so much a personal repentance, perhaps, as a hopeless cultural regret.'

He came to a place which had just been bombed. Jagged shards of metal were embedded in tree trunks, blued by intense heat, cauterising the wounds they made. The air reeked of high explosive, something like fart and pepper. Not a bird called. Chunks of red laterite still detached themselves from the craters' lips and rolled towards the bottom, smoking. After ten months in the jungle he knew that smell from a distance. Even with the blindfold on he could recognise the scent of punished landscape, the sap and boiled earth. There seemed no point to the damage. The Major was accustomed to the fighter pilot's honed view: precise targets on which cannon fire, missiles, or even shiny napalm canisters converged. But this strategic bombing of a jungle in no country he could define felt less like an inaccurate weapon than an inaccurate war. Still he clung to his name, rank and number even though by now he was getting the gist of some of the words which flew past him like shrapnel.

On the fringes of bombed areas immediately after a strike it was sometimes possible to find dead or injured animals such as snakes, monkeys, tree lizards and birds, all of which his captors would eagerly roast. The Major's treatment had now risen to that of a dog, tossed the odd bone with a benign indifference. He had been inherited by different captors often enough for his ex-combatant status to have worn off. His clothes were so filthy and ragged, his head so bearded and thatched, that the knight of the air had vanished into a wild man of the woods, a species of feral mascot tugged behind on a light cord. And still he wouldn't speak except to mutter his name and rank and number.

One evening they came to the edge of a citrus grove. The Major was done for, his feet bleeding. He collapsed in a faint at the foot of a tree. He was woken by a soldier who brought him a bowl of music. The Major drank and his head cleared a little and still he heard the music. It was the sound of a piano. In the dusk, among the frogs and lizards calling, someone was playing Bach. He stared at the bowl. 'I'm hallucinating,' he told the boy. 'I can't last.' 'No, no,' the boy urged him. 'It's real. Just listen.'

How could it be real? At the end of a trail winding for months into the heart of Indochina how could there be a piano? Two soldiers manhandled him to his feet and pushed him through the trees, stumbling over roots. Steadier lights appeared among the fireflies: the white rectangles of the windows lit by electricity. The music grew louder. At the steps of a neat bungalow the soldiers halted. The Major sat down, strength gone, and leaned his head against the cement balustrade. Somebody inside the house or else inside his head was playing the First Partita. The music rolled over him and flooded out into the orchard. As it did so all incongruity vanished. The swept and beaten earth around the bungalow, the rusting Milo tins with flowering shrubs in them, the unseen military men patrolling the shadows, the flicker of fruit bats around a palm tree's head: all fell beneath the spell and were tamed into normality. He felt his fragments start to congeal around this forgotten sound. Time rewound itself. Somewhere in the distance a generator softly thudded.

After a while the weeping Major looked up. In the silence a trim European with white hair was watching from the veranda.

'Won't you come up?' asked this man in accented English. 'I'm sure you'd like to wash before dinner.'

Incredulously, the Major found himself helped beneath a shower, fumbling with freed hands a bar of soap whose scent pierced him nearly as much as Bach had. Then he was sitting at a table wearing a silk dressing-gown, blinking in the unaccustomed light, while a girl in an *ao dai* served him food such as he had dreamed about obsessively. The weight of cutlery in his hands slowed them to a semblance of table manners. Instead of scooping the fluffy rice up with a hand and plastering it into the hole in his beard the Major managed to restrain himself though he ate with terrible concentration, glaring at the food as it disappeared. At length his host asked:

'Better?'

'Oh God.' Then, warily, 'Who are you?'

'Darius Fauchon.'

'They're keeping you here? Where in hell are we?'

The European smiled. 'I was born here. I'm a simple planter. This place is called Can Tau. And who are you?'

The Major blinked and his mouth stumbled on his name, rank and number without its usual fluency. He had to think. 'You're French, right?'

'My parents were French,' his host told him. 'Naturally, since I was born here, I am Vietnamese.'

'I didn't know the Vietnamese played Bach.'

'You recognised it?'

'I used to play it myself, years ago.'

The Major felt himself expand as the unaccustomed food and wine took hold.

'Oh!' exclaimed Fauchon with pleasure. 'You're a pianist too? I'm only an amateur, of course, but you're like a dream come true. At last I've someone to play duets with. You really must stay now that you're here. Do you by any chance know Schubert's four-hand music?'

The Major, who felt gorged, had in fact eaten little. He allowed himself to be helped to a couch, whereupon another girl in an *ao dai* appeared with a bowl and some towels and began bathing his cracked feet with herbal tinctures. She patted them carefully dry and put dressings on his wounds. The knight lay back, bemused, not able to speak, hypnotised by the slowly revolving blades of the ceiling fan. His host meanwhile kept up a steady conversation with a middle-aged man in peasant clothes who had wandered in. They might have been discussing the ground-nut harvest for all the Major knew or cared. The war had vanished. His captors were presumably lurking in the groves around the house, ready to come in and pinion his arms and wander him off again as soon as this bizarre interlude was over. At length, though, he and the Frenchman were left alone.

'Where's the war?' he asked bitterly. The last year's sufferings seemed after all to have been unnecessary.

'Oh, dragging on, you know.' The Frenchman made a dismissive gesture. 'You're probably a bit behind with the news. Your countrymen are none too happy about things. Opposition seems to be growing back home: student protests, draft dodging, riots, all that. As you've no doubt deduced by now, the war doesn't after all seem to be about what you were told it was about. Little is, when you come to think of it.'

Without warning the man went to seat himself at the piano and began to play one of the 'Forty-Eight' preludes. Bemused, the Major once again found himself reduced to tears. This was a way stage on a lethal trek, a short break like an unexpected split in a heavy overcast allowing a glimpse of the eternal bright blue wrapping the planet. Where fighter pilots flew and Bach lived there was no weather. Suddenly the possibility of staying alive was hugely precious. Yokes, privations, leeches and beatings could be survived or even – if one played one's hand as smartly as this French planter appeared to have – avoided entirely. Being a knight was not the only way of spending a life. Evidently this man's own father had had entirely different expectations for his son. What was considered an honourable way to live varied greatly according to something as flimsy as local fashion . . . Meanwhile the music filled him, each note falling like a drop of rain into his parched soul. His weakened mind became crowded with banalities and ravishment; with the banality of ravishment.

Some time later he heard his mouth talking. It seemed to have been doing it for a long time. The Frenchman was sitting turned to face him on the piano stool, nodding now and then as an analyst might, encouraging the weight to leave the mind without improper eliciting. The Major told of the horrors he'd seen, the Montagnard villages burnt out, the shredded bodies of mountain folk who had no more to do with this foreigners' war than ants have with the descending boot heel. He told of jungle fastnesses full of strange and beautiful creatures erased to vapour and craters. A year's unexpressed pain leached out of him. He spoke on and on in a sad monotone in that bright and civilised room to his bright and civilised host who from time to time simply turned round and played the piano for a few minutes by way of punctuation. Whenever he did the Major's eyes filled hopelessly with tears, though the former knight of so many months ago would have *known* there would probably be a film camera turning silently behind an aperture at the back of the bookshelves which directly faced him.

The Last of the Habsburgs

DISASTER LOOMED in the stricken, war-torn and disputed Enclave. Its territorial waters, sadly unoiled and hence troubled, were further marred by violence as negotiations got under way, towing a raft of new measures. In the distance a large question-mark hung over blocks of stumble which in turn were themselves hanging in the balance above a key crossroads. Underneath them, a concrete aid package was on the table. At grassroots level allegations were mushrooming, among which rebel factions held pea-stalks, while in a race against time hard-pressed surgeons performed delicate face-saving and fence-mending operations.

'Well, if the BBC says so it must be true,' Pikel Tarza thought to himself, sitting up in bed and turning off his short-wave radio. 'They're listened to the world over. I must admit they paint a gloomy picture. I hadn't realised things were so bad in the provinces.'

In the Enclave's capital, all unbeknownst to the BBC, it was the eve of a week's festivities commemorating the bicentenary of the death of the National Composer, Lugo

Pirbit (1729–1795). Excitement was considerable, to a large degree taking its cue from the King himself. Vazimil III was an enthusiastic amateur musician in the tradition of Frederick the Great and Archduke Rudolph and he had ordered no expense spared to do justice to Pirbit's sublime legacy. It had fallen to Pikel Tarza as Kapellmeister to organise the various concerts and recitals which would take place all over town throughout the week, culminating in Sunday evening's grand programme in the cathedral. On that night everyone of any consequence in the Enclave would be there; and for as long as the concert lasted the nation would (with the exception of the surreal goings-on in the provinces) come to a festive halt.

Kapellmeister Tarza's task had not been easy and preparations had begun almost a year ago. The logistics of arranging who went when to which hall to play what music had been bad enough, but devising the final night's programme had been tricky indeed. The great Pirbit's famous recalcitrance had easily survived two centuries. Ahead of his times in many things, he had been a devout satanist and had written a series of black masses of which the last, *Missa nigra solennissima* in D, was reckoned his masterpiece in the genre. It had been the King's own preference for this climactic concert, but the Patriarch had been quite firm. Pirbit or not, it was a most improper choice for any part of the ceremonies and absolutely out of the question in the cathedral. At first the King had been taken aback. An entirely secular man, he hadn't until that moment made any connection between the piece and the place. To him it was simply a marvellous composition displaying to the full the thrilling blending of two musical traditions, the Austrian Catholicism of Haydn's day with Eastern Orthodoxy. ('I can't help that,' the Patriarch had said. 'There'll be no anathemas in *my* cathedral.')

So that was no good. After much negotiation the King and Tarza had agreed on a programme whose innocuous first half consisted of an overture, a couple of symphonies and Pirbit's ever-popular balalaika concerto. The King was disposed to be a little snobbish about the last item but Tarza had insisted it was a necessary sop to the public in view of the programme's second half. For this the King had decided on something very special indeed: the first-ever performance of Pirbit's unfinished opera *Habsza-brugye Khust* (The Last of the Habsburgs) in which he himself proposed to sing the role of Othmar the King. On first learning of this audacious plan Tarza's dismay, loyally concealed, had been acute. It was no accident that the piece had never been staged: it was a mere torso with only a few numbers completed and the rest barely sketched out by the dying composer. Some of the sketches were in short score but most were on single staves interspersed with his own illegible reminders to himself. There was more than enough music to show that Pirbit was still at the height of his powers, however, which but added to the already poignant aura that always hung about a great artist's last work. The problem of the text was one

thing, Pikel Tarza thought ruefully; the King as singer was
something else. It was not that the Vazimil voice was
particularly bad. He had a pleasant bass whose once-shaky
upper register had been worked on and much improved
by a series of foreigners. What he lacked was a sense of
rhythm. He simply couldn't count. Tarza had once read a
description of Frederick the Great's flute-playing by one of
his Court musicians – Quantz or C.P.E. Bach or someone
– who said that it was fine so long as the music was slow,
but in fast movements accompanying him was an art in
itself. This was all too true of King Vazimil, who would
cheerfully shave off or add the odd bar as the fervour took
him. One forgave him much, Tarza thought, because he
was a genuinely nice man and he really tried, as well as
being a generous employer. But to choose *Habszabrugye
Khust*, of all things . . . ! Mercifully the role of King
Othmar, such of it as had been written, was not large. It
was confined to a single aria and several grave Sarastro-like
utterances pregnant with wisdom, dignity and so forth.
There were a couple of excuses for hitting a *basso profondo*
bottom C which Vazimil could do with relish and ease. It
sounded like a squeezed ox.

The foremost Pirbit scholar had been coerced into
producing a performable version of the opera from the
sketches. He and Tarza had worked on the orchestration
together and the result, when they'd played the whole
thing through as a piano duet with their own falsetto
accompaniment, was really not bad at all. It wasn't

Deryck Cooke's Mahler Ten, and Pirbit might be turning in his grave, but at least his final work would be getting an airing. Besides, it was an interesting piece in its own right. One would have been hard pushed to describe Pirbit's eclectic and highly individual musical style other than to say it suggested a J. M. Kraus brought up on the wrong side of the Carpathians. As for the opera's libretto, the composer had written it himself and it was full of his own cross-grained radicalism.

The plot was simple enough. It is the day of Othmar's Coronation in 1795. A sensitive man, he is conscious of the waves of republicanism eddying around Europe in the wake of the French Revolution, and even more acutely aware that Louis XVI has not long since been guillotined in Paris. Not entirely for reasons of cowardice he wishes to make it clear to the people that though he is about to become their monarch he intends to rule them with humility and enlightenment. Meanwhile Konrad, a popular demagogue, is threatening to raise a mob to disrupt the Coronation. In a dramatic scene the future king sternly forbids his chief-of-staff to arrest Konrad and generally break heads in the customary fashion. To the contrary, argues Othmar in a lengthy *recitativo secco*, he and his mob must be invited to the cathedral to witness the ceremony for themselves. It is only right that the governed should see their governor pledge allegiance equally to God and their welfare. The chief-of-staff retires, shaking his head at this early and ominous sign of weakness. The Coronation service goes ahead and Konrad duly interrupts the proceedings before Othmar can be crowned. The guards of honour are hopelessly outnumbered and the mob surges into the cathedral unhindered. Othmar faces them alone in his regalia before the high altar and, in a *coup de théâtre*, raises his jewelled hand. They fall silent, overawed. He tells them they are right, all this panoply of majesty is just theatre. Beneath the ermine and velvet and brocade is a human being like themselves, a naked mortal. There is no divine right of kings: royal blood guarantees nothing more than a certain kind of training, and even this counts for little if the man is unworthy of the throne. Then comes the opera's most audacious moment, when Othmar invites Konrad to take his place and be crowned in his stead. In the incredulous hush which falls his cronies push the reluctant Konrad in his jerkin and stout breeches slowly forward to the vacant throne. Suddenly a laugh rings out, followed by others; the laughter spreads until the entire cathedral is rocking with mirth. Again Othmar raises his hand for silence and then lets it fall gently on to the trembling Konrad's shoulder. '*Spradi burot y'min*', Stay, my friend, he sings in his great aria and Konrad sinks to his knees. When Othmar is crowned at last the demagogue becomes the first to swear the oath of allegiance to his sovereign, which is the signal for a flourish on the organ and a final chorus of thanksgiving and rejoicing.

It was just as well Pirbit had never finished this seditious extravaganza. In 1795 there would have been precious little chance of his seeing it staged and every likelihood of his disappearing into one of the many Janissary dungeons which then dotted the Enclave. But in 1995 Pikel Tarza and King Vazimil thought it struck just the right note: loweringly democratic and then reassuringly traditional, with mystical hints and some jolly good tunes.

And now the great commemorative Pirbit Week was about to start, with everything rehearsed to perfection and the King gargling six times a day with a solution of myrrh in arak. On the eve of the opening concerts Pikel Tarza went to track down some instrumental parts in the Imperial Music Library and had found the copies he was looking for, somewhat war-torn but quite legible, when he ran into the King, empty glass in hand, in the Royal Music Schools. Vazimil gave the scores a keen glance.

'All set, eh, Tarza?'

'Absolutely, Highness. I trust your throat is giving no cause for alarm?'

'Oh no, it's fine. Just following doctor's orders. Tell me, Tarza,' said the King earnestly, 'you understand political things. What exactly *is* an enclave? I gathered from the BBC this morning that we're one.'

'According to the dictionary in the British Council library, Highness, it's somewhere that's completely enclosed within a foreign territory. It's from the Latin *in* and *clavis*, a key.'

'You mean we're cut off? My field marshals have said nothing about it. How peculiar. You'd think they would have mentioned it.'

'Still, Highness, the BBC. Its accuracy is widely held to be unimpeachable.'

'So we're isolated, are we? What with all this wonderful music I can't say I've been paying too much attention to external affairs. Some very odd things do seem to be happening, though. Apparently there's a table out there somewhere with a package of new measures on it. I distinctly heard it. I can't imagine why the BBC should think it worth mentioning. One assumes the Metrication Board ordered them, or the Department of Surveys. Well, well, *in* and *clavis*, eh? I suppose one could say the second movement of that symphony you're holding's an enclave in A flat. Entirely surrounded by E flat, I mean.'

'That's extremely witty, Highness.'

'Oh and Tarza, do you happen to know the name of the dialect the BBC is using nowadays? Is it the King's or the Queen's English?'

'I really couldn't say, Sire. I think it may be European English since they joined the Union.'

'It's very colourful. Most picturesque and graphic. Far more so than the old style they used to have which was plain and dull. I hope little Prince Tassil is taught it when he goes to Harro next year. Harro Academy,' said the King wistfully. 'I wonder if they still beat boys as hard as they did when I was there? Some people grow to like it, I understand,' he added disingenuously. 'They find it quite a tonic to be in the subdominant, as it were.'

As it were indeed, thought Pikel Tarza as he hurried off

with the scores under his arm. Obviously the old boy was in fine form: his musical puns were a reliable barometer of his spirits. With any luck he wouldn't go to pieces on Sunday and *Habszabrugye* would be a grand success. It was a significant musical occasion, after all: the première of a 200-year-old opera and staged in a real cathedral. Theatre in the round, with Konrad and the mob extras pouring in from the west door and the orchestra crowded into the organ loft. It would knock spots off anything ever done at Eszterháza. As Kapellmeister, Tarza had taken it upon himself to invite H. C. Robbins Landon to this historic performance and was still hoping for a reply.

In the event, National Pirbit Week went off flawlessly. At the King's request all the major concerts were broadcast over the radio so no-one in his tiny nation need feel deprived. The BBC noticed this almost at once and by Monday evening were announcing in their droll way that Radio Enclave had abruptly gone off the air and its programmes had been replaced by solemn music. As the days passed the picture they drew of events in the provinces became ever more vivid yet ever more obscure. It was almost as though immediately beyond the capital's outskirts the light dimmed to a menacing dusk in which a series of tableaux was enacted, Daliesque juxtapositions of objects stranded in a combat zone. Pikel Tarza was far too preoccupied with the music festival to pay it much heed but he did register that out in the countryside it was once again the season for agendas to be pursued and earmarked.

Another year gone! How time sped by when one was busy! The reports left him vaguely uneasy and he decided that as soon as the opera was over on Sunday night he would ask someone knowledgeable what on earth was going on. It was the impression of waning light that most worried him. Out there hopes were rapidly fading and terms and deals were constantly having to be spelled out. Addresses too, presumably, which would have made a postman's job (for example) extremely trying and would explain the open-ended packages lying about the land-scape, one of which apparently belonged to a locksmith and must have been urgent for it was described as a key package which somebody was rushing to finalise.

Yet none of this weird confusion touched the capital, which was sunny and warm and full of people sitting with glasses of wine at little tin tables while a band played endless sets of Pirbit's minuets and contredanses. Towards the end of the week some of the younger citizens, in particular, were betraying signs of having heard enough of Lugo Pirbit's music to last them the next two hundred years, so by the time Sunday came there was a national sense of both expectation and relief. The great Byzantine cathedral in the historic city centre was jammed an hour before the concert was scheduled to begin and little Prince Tassil entertained the waiting audience with a pot-pourri of Pirbit's simpler organ works. These were for manuals only, which was why he could play them: his slippered feet swung three inches above the pedal board. After an adroit half-hour recital he was helped down off the bench to great applause.

Punctually at seven o'clock the main concert began. The overture to 'The Millionaire Shepherd', Pirbit's excellent *opera buffa*, was successfully followed by two of his later symphonies, opp. 167 and 171. The audience listened with quiet pleasure, but it was clearly the balalaika concerto they were waiting for and they awarded the soloist a standing ovation both before and after his glittering performance. Then came the interval which gave time for all those involved in the opera to change into their costumes as well as for a few props to be carried on, including a throne of gilded oak.

Meanwhile, outside in the precincts' ancient alleys and piazzas the extras had been assembling, roughly costumed. Konrad the demagogue roamed nervously among them sucking menthol bonbons, occasionally grimacing and massaging his throat before essaying a loud *Fah-ah-ah-ah!* on ascending notes or *Ti-ti-ti-ti!* in his vibrant heroic tenor. Pitchforks and cudgels glinted in the setting sun. Children munched salted melon seeds and played with yo-yos. Their mothers, squeezed into hastily run-up bodices of vaguely eighteenth-century cut, fanned themselves and tried not to breathe too deeply. And suddenly from within the cathedral the first chords of the opera's overture could be heard. *Habszabrugye Khust* had started at last.

It was a triumph. As far as the audience was concerned it had everything: drama, action, the King himself in a starring role and – above all – brevity, since the entire score ran to just under the hour. They loved it. The mob had been well drilled and invaded the cathedral with just the right degree of sinister belligerence, spitting melon seed husks and packing the side aisles while down the nave strode Konrad in leather jerkin and fierce mustachios, a balsa wood cudgel in one fist and trailing a strong smell of menthol. His subduing by wise King Othmar held everyone spellbound. Not a person there missed the dramatic irony of seeing Vazimil III impersonating a monarch whose enlightenment wins for his people liberation from the dark threat of mob rule. It was more than a resurrected opera, it was a timely parable; and many an eye sparkled with unshed tears. One of the most moving moments came when the King with a single raised hand stopped the tumultuous laughter at Konrad's expense. Behind the laughter the organ and orchestra had been getting louder and louder on a pedal point in the dominant and when the King held up his hand and an echoing silence fell for five seconds the music, having reached a key crossroads, hung a right into the tonic and Vazimil launched into his affecting aria, 'Stay my friend'. He sang it surprisingly well and Pikel Tarza, who was conducting and had been dreading this very moment, managed without difficulty to keep orchestra and soloist together. At the King's final repetition of '*Spradi burot y'min*' many in the audience were weeping openly.

While this drama was being played out in the cathedral

the BBC was busy giving its listeners its own account of events as they developed in the disputed Enclave. A reporter, lurking in the streets of the capital, was bouncing messages off a satellite to the effect that a heavily armed mob had been seen to converge on the cathedral where it was known King Vazimil was attending a service. Tension was mounting. Shouts and then laughter had been heard to drown out the sound of music within. At the moment when Othmar was being crowned King the reporter announced that confusion was reigning in the capital, and in a further happy coincidence added that obscurity now surrounded the King's whereabouts. At that very instant this was no less than the truth since Vazimil was standing beneath a single spotlight in the dramatically darkened cathedral.

None of this was of the least consequence to the Enclave's citizens since nobody was at home listening to their short-wave radios. *Habszabrugye* drew to its grand close and the audience, many of whom had sung along with the final chorus despite not knowing the music, burst into patriotic cheering and prolonged applause which the smiling Patriarch readily forgave. What was God's house for if not for the occasional expression of joy? Two hours later, with the cathedral emptied and the happy crowds dispersed, King Vazimil, still a-tremble with his delirious success, at last stopped breaking into fragments of his aria and collapsed into an overstuffed armchair. In due course his exhausted Kapellmeister was able to totter away to his

own apartment and firmly shut the door. The week had
been a triumph after all. Lugo Pirbit had been well and truly
served and Pikel Tarza had just been proclaimed a
Companion of the Golden Clef, an order which the King
had invented on the spot and which carried a lavish pension.

'We'll work out a heraldic device tomorrow,' Vazimil
had burbled. 'It'll all tie neatly together in one design, just
you see. A treble clef, *clavis*, a key, wholly surrounded by
an Enclave *or*.'

Swiftly Tarza undressed and sank into bed, his head still
ringing with music. From force of habit he switched on
the radio and, as he dozed off, once more found himself
transported by the BBC to that twilit zone which
stretched out there beyond the capital. In the dusk-filled
distance some sinister figures were obscurely busy. There
was menace in the way their arms rhythmically rose and
fell. At length he thought he could see what they were
doing. They were dashing hopes against a tariff barrier in
defiance of the authorities who stood leaning impotently
on their brooms, their sweeping powers temporarily
exhausted. In the shadow cast by a nearby wall of silence
he could make out the figure of a BBC reporter watching.
Pikel Tarza felt sorry for him that he'd missed the concert:
the opera really had been splendid as well as full of interest
and significance for Enclave-watchers. But the man just
went on standing there in his headphones, impervious as
ever to the Enclave's cultural life, his spectacles lit by the
eerie twinkle of flashpoints.

Bambi Bar

THE NIGHTCLUB itself was confined to the ground floor but the thud of its music and the singers' wails permeated the rest of the building. On the floor above were vague areas for the hostesses, performers and the band strewn with elasticated Bambi tails, satiny costumes, make-up boxes, knickers, an electric guitar or two, a chair surrounded by the scattered tufts of an impromptu haircut. Congealing cups of coffee and a row of empty San Miguel beer bottles stood on the window-sill overlooking the gridlocked street. The view outside was of the gimcrack façades of the bars and clubs opposite and the battered tin rectangles of jeepney roofs down below jammed together as higgledy-piggledy as crazy paving. Traffic noise beat up through the glass. Amplified bass notes tingled the floor, sending up spurts of dust from between the boards. A further flight up were the club's offices as well as a couple of plywood rooms kept for the odd high-rolling patron who had nowhere else to take his Bambi girl. If the police ever happened by, they were told the rooms were where the singers slept in between acts, though no singer would ever dare sleep there and risk being caught by the club's owner, Mrs Tan.

Even up here the music was audible. To escape it the singers would go right on up to the flat roof where, among the TV antennae and rusty air extractor trunking from the kitchen, lengths of reed matting had been rigged into a shade. Beneath it the girls crawled on to mats and slept, wrapped in cotton blankets against the cockroaches and the soot which rose in clouds from the traffic four floors down. Then they were shaken awake, stumbled down-stairs again (quick squirt of breath freshener, thicken up the lashes) and on to the tiny stage, a bit of brain still stranded back home in the provinces where sleep had abandoned them.

'Dulce! Dulce! *Hoy, gising*! You're on in five.'

'What's the time?'

'Two-fifteen.'

The bright sunlight of her home village overlaid the strobes and neons of nightbound Manila, fading them to a dreamscape. Still within its radiance, she tripped onstage into the freezing cockpit with its air-conditioned reek, the chilled smoke and beer fumes. Danny Alonzo would wink and give her a riff on his keyboard and she would be off into 'The Sunny Side of the Street' even as she half expected to hear her voice launch of its own accord into 'Mayong pinagpala' or 'Santa Elena' or another of her favourite Flores de Mayo songs.

'I'm so tired, Danny.'

'Don't moan, kid. It's the same for all of us. You'll get used to it. All you have to do is sing and waggle your parts. Thank your lucky stars you're not a hostess.'

'*All* they do is waggle. They don't have to sing as well. And nobody really listens to your voice, do they? It's just background noise.'

'They listen. Old Lettie was saying only this morning the word's getting around, people are coming here on purpose to listen to you. Quite the little high-flyer. You've got talent, Dulce. *I've* got talent. We're waiting for a break, okay? We've a long way to go. Bambi Bar's just the first stop. It pays the rent.'

'Sure, Danny. I know.' She would give his hand a grateful squeeze which Danny returned encouragingly, protectively. For it seemed as though all the performers felt protective towards Dulce. Although half of them were themselves nice girls from the provinces trying to hack it in the big bad city they knew she was different, even more vulnerable than they. The ruefully generous among them would also admit she was more talented. She could pick up a song at a single hearing and her voice had a rounded purity which, out of place as it was in Bambi Bar, suggested sensibility. Her chief regret was that she didn't have a fraction of the money for proper voice lessons, still less for the college music course she would have loved.

Dulce was always whacked when she went home at around five in the morning, regardless of how much sleep she'd managed to snatch in between acts. Yet as soon as she got off the jeepney and began walking the last few blocks something awoke in her which spread a sad alertness throughout her body. At that hour and in this residential area traffic noise was limited to the occasional car passing unseen in the surrounding streets. Cats and rats were at work in heaps of rubbish and, behind high walls, a palm or a papaya could be glimpsed here and there outlined against the paling sky. A fresh breeze, too, might be drifting in from the seafront only eight blocks over, rattling the fronds and easing away the city's soot and monoxides towards Laguna. It blew into Dulce's heart a crippling homesickness for the village by the sea where her family were even then – according to her Chinese quartz watch – up and about. Beneath little squares of rusty tin the first *bibingka*s would be rising and browning in their clay dishes, wreathed in the fragrance of charcoal and baking. Sleeping mats would be rolled and stowed while from outside the house would come the sound of Marisil's brush strokes as she swept fallen leaves, sweet wrappers and cigarette packets into heaps for burning. Dulce could see the various efforts to wake her oldest brother Noriel, who was about to graduate from high school. He would still be curled up in the room he'd curtained off for himself beneath the stairs, the lazy pig, surrounded by posters of the film actresses he fancied and the electronic stuffing from various radios and Walkmans he'd undertaken to repair. Her eyes filled with tears at the vividness of the picture, at the certain knowledge that these things were actually happening at this very moment in a place far away, that she was seeing and smelling and hearing a reality in which she was only an absence. '*Ay, na sa Maynila si Dulce.*' How clearly she could hear the phrase with its mixture of pride and hopefulness and apprehension. Maybe by dint of hard work and luck she could change her family's fortunes. Maybe with a Guardian Angel's protection she could avoid the profusion of horrid fates which danced attendance on country girls who went to Manila.

As Dulce reached her rented lodgings her nostalgia was compounded by guilt. She hadn't dared tell her parents where she was working. Not that she'd actually lied in her letters home; rather, she'd blurred the business of her work in such a way as to leave the impression that she was a singer in one of the city's international hotels: the Ramada or the Hilton, the Hyatt or Holiday Inn. To have confessed to Bambi Bar in Pasay would have been a truthfulness which could only have led to endless worry and disappointment. She let herself in, amazed as usual that no-one was stirring. People here in the city certainly kept very different hours. Upstairs the double row of cubicle doorways showed no activity other than the curtains billowing and shuddering to the draught of electric fans. She went into her own plywood cell and shook awake fat Lerma, the cook's daughter, who otherwise would have had to sleep on the floor downstairs with the cockroaches. Lerma, who was fourteen, came awake without a sound, stared at Dulce from sodden eyes, slowly

wrapped her sheet around her and still without a word
padded barefoot out of the cubicle like an obedient
mummy. Next to the bed was a tea-chest covered in
printed cotton which served as a table and Dulce could see
at a glance that Lerma had left behind some elastic hair-
bands and a squeeze bottle of body lotion by Charmis
called 'Frenzy'. Somewhere down in the kitchen regions a
cock crowed. She wanted a shower but was too tired.
Besides, she could now hear sounds of movement from
the other cubicles and couldn't face the competitive
queuing and impatient door-poundings involved in eleven
other girls all trying to use the two cement stalls
downstairs at the same time, morning ablutions made
desperately against the clock. No, far better to bathe later
when she awoke and the house was practically empty.
Besides, maybe by then there'd be a letter from home. She
might even write to Noriel, newly emboldened by
Danny's secondhand compliments. People were actually
coming to hear her sing, then? And was she really getting a
reputation as a high-flyer? Wrapping herself in her own
blanket Dulce fell asleep on the slat bed as around her the
other cubicles sprang to life and the girls, duly showered
and smelling of Camay and Lifebuoy and Tawas, arrayed
themselves variously in their uniforms as college students,
shop assistants, nurses and office workers. From downstairs drifted the smell of frying fish and the sound of the
TV in the passageway.

– Dulce, Dulce – her Guardian Angel might have

whispered as she slept. – My dear, my sister, my love. What is this great plan of yours that you throw yourself into my protection, yield your only life into my hands? –

But there was no plan, not as such. In a way it was negative planning based on the idea that if one had a talent it had no future in the provinces. Nothing ever happened in the provinces and nothing ever would, except predictable things such as pregnancy and marriage. By going to Manila one was at least putting oneself in the path of change, into the way of a remote possibility where luck might strike, a gift be recognised, a job be offered with a salary large enough for remittances to be sent home. This negative planning – or positive wishful thinking – brought young people flocking to the city each year in their tens of thousands, the great majority of whom had far less reason than Dulce to feel they merited the touch of luck's wand.

For Dulce really did have talent and had always done the best she could to develop it. Ever since elementary school she had wanted to be a singer. As she grew up a difference became apparent between herself and all the other local girls who planned to be singers. What they really wanted, she thought, was to be there in the spotlight, the centre of attention. It wouldn't much matter to them what they were doing; some of them (she considered bleakly and disloyally) might as well become strippers as singers. They read the fanzines avidly, followed all the stories about Vangie this, Sharon that, Dawn the other, Vic, Gloria, Lorna. They were gripped by the mythmaking of showbiz and filmland where romances were larger than life, success was measured on the Richter scale, and fortunes were too huge to be worth counting. Dulce, too, read the same magazines, but her secret was of a different sort and she kept it hidden from all but her closest friends. It was that she loved the songs themselves more than the singers and wanted in turn to sing them because it was the best way she had of expressing her love. If ever she yearned to be up there onstage in the spotlights it was because she wanted other people to hear the songs, to feel that lift which came when a tune really got into your bones and made your whole body hum. She couldn't imagine having a mood for which no song suggested itself. There was no aspect of life which couldn't be sung.

Since well before her teens Dulce had been involved in nearly every village activity which required music, especially in the school and church hidden among the palms. By the time she was twelve she was also the best guitar player in the village, which gave her a curious and faintly uneasy status. The fact was that women didn't play the guitar. There was no law or taboo against it – they simply didn't do it. As most of the village's guitar playing went on at the men's nightly drinking sessions it would hardly have been a seemly activity for a teenage girl, so the men continued to play badly for each other and were probably too drunk to care. However, the idea of a girl playing the guitar was all right as long as she did it for the choir in church or something similar, so it became generally agreed that

Dulce was religious – might even have lapsed out of her native Catholicism into some sort of evangelism. Weren't the Born-Agains famously given to sing-songs with guitars and suchlike, wholesome ditties about walking tall with Jesus?

But Dulce wasn't religious. Or, if she were, she remained a Catholic. No, she just loved singing and had skills whose outlet was in the local musical activities, most of which had religious roots such as the youth choirs sponsored by the diocesan council. By fifteen she was much in demand and spent a good deal of her time going with Father Ben's group to sing for a christening here, a wedding there, for confirmations and masses and speech days and convocations and Holy Week retreats and youth festivals in towns and villages up and down the coast. 'Everyone loves a musician,' Father Ben said more than once. 'Music will make you friends wherever you go.'

'Music, my arse,' her brother Noriel would gibe affectionately. 'Boy-mad, more like. As long as they've got half a voice and the price of a Coke. *Aruy!*' as a plastic bottle of Green Cross rubbing alcohol glanced off his shoulder. Dodging, he called out: 'What's his name? The skinny one? Perfecto? *Ay*, Pecto, Pecto! Wow legs!'

But that wasn't true, either, as Noriel well knew. Dulce had no lack of suitors and in fact was spoiled for choice, being both talented and pretty. Deftly she played them off one against the other, committing herself to none while somehow managing not to acquire the reputation of being a flirt. Again, she probably achieved this by being so obviously preoccupied with her music, her singing, as to leave little time for mundane adolescent activities.

'She's young yet,' her mother would say defensively to the other women as they crouched in the river shallows with their skirts hitched up, working through piles of washing and gossiping. 'Dulce's going to go far.'

'Not in the husband stakes, unless she wakes up.'

'I expect my daughter'll marry when she's good and ready, Sita. She's barely sixteen. At least she's not so hungry she's reduced to being a vegetarian.'

Howls of laughter from the others greeted this riposte since it referred to Teresita's own daughter who, according to rumour, had recently strayed down to the beach with her basket of bitter cucumbers where some youths were busy digging sand for hollow blocks. To her hawker's cry of 'Bitter cucumbers!' Tino had famously replied 'Try my sweet one, darling', and there wasn't a washerwoman in the village who didn't believe that later, under cover of darkness, she had.

'I'm sure you're right,' Teresita agreed, 'when you say Dulce will go far. All the way to Japan, probably, as a Japayuki.'

These morning sallies, accompanied by the echoing blows of wooden paddles on sodden lumps of washing together with screams of laughter, greatly invigorated all concerned and made the time fly. Fickle conversational currents of enmity and alliance swirled around as the river slid placidly past, carrying away eroding floes of suds to the sea. Yet jokes and gossip often had a curious habit of fulfilling themselves, of becoming true as much from an unsuspected accuracy as from the power of spite. Within a month or two Dulce found herself drawn to Perfecto, who was by no means as skinny as her brother had said. The more she became involved in the music of the diocese, the more she saw of him. He lived in the town six miles away, a serious, quiet boy who could be relied on to sit up all night by candlelight copying out song sheets for the choir when the only Xerox machine for miles had broken or run out of toner. He was said to be thinking of going into the Church and spent a good deal of his time with Father Ben. One day when he and she were planning the next month's rehearsals she asked him one of those questions that only the very young can ask without banality.

'What do you want, Pecto? In your life?'

A million other teenagers would have said something like 'Oh, happiness, I suppose.' 'True love.' 'A good job, some land of my own and a family.' Perfecto replied 'Truthfulness.' Just that.

'Truthfulness?'

'Accuracy, then. In everything, I mean. I hate it when things are blurred. Like in choir when someone's not sure of the part and the harmony's not quite clean.'

'And your motives, Pecto? Are they quite clean?'

He turned away in confusion, lashes lowered.

'I didn't mean that,' Dulce said hurriedly. 'I'm sorry.'

'No, you're quite right. You truthfully wanted to know and already I'm failing my own standards. I admit it. My motives are blurred. My faith is blurred. My singing is blurred.'

'Too hard on yourself,' Dulce told him affectionately. From then on they became closer, walking along the beach together after school but only while it was still light enough to provoke chaffing rather than rumour.

'I love your voice, Dulce,' he said. 'It's the sound of your own truthfulness because it expresses you so well. You can only become a singer, can't you? I mean, you're already a singer. I wish I were, but I'm not. I just sing.'

'You sing very well, Pecto.'

But he gave her an impatient look as though he couldn't be bothered with the muddiness of social nicety. Within months Father Ben had been posted eighty miles away and Dulce was officially appointed choirleader. A girl in charge of the choir . . . It was unheard of. Now she and Perfecto were constantly in each other's company, organising, practising, copying, singing, confiding; especially confiding. ('We're too young for romance,' Dulce would tell herself at night, lying on her bed and staring up at the thatched roof faintly lit by the tiny glow of a wick stuck in a mayonnaise jar of oil. From under the stairs came Noriel's snores; from outside sudden outbursts of barking as the village dogs prowled and marauded, and in the silences the call of a gecko, the ocean's gasps.) But even as she thought it she knew she wasn't too young at all, while having to admit she couldn't imagine Pecto lying awake six miles away worrying that he might fall in love with her. *Confiding* was right. You felt you could tell him anything, things too private for one's best friend or mother or elder sister. Yet he managed to be intimate without being romantic. It was because he was going to be a priest, she thought. It's a priest's mode. Absolute sincerity, absolute secrecy, oddly unjudgmental. He confided in her, too, even quite intimate confessions of jealousies and fears, putting himself into her hands in a way she thought of as erotic until she realised there always remained something he wouldn't tell her. A part of him stayed closed, as if he had no words to express it; you sensed it there even when he was being honest to his own detriment, as if its hidden presence was exactly what gave him the freedom to confess to anything else. This, Dulce imagined, was what it meant to be deeply religious.

– Dulce, Dulce, – said her Guardian Angel one night after a year. – There is nothing to happen. There are many different kinds of love. His is different entirely. –

'It's time to go,' she thought, suddenly both miserable and excited.

– I didn't say that – said her Angel in alarm. – Dear Dulce, don't do anything rash. You're safe here, and loved. –

'Too safe, and not enough loved,' said Dulce bravely, and within the month had announced to her family that she had written to Cousin Lita to ask if she could stay with her in Parañaque while looking for a job in the city. When she told Pecto his eyes filled with tears.

'You too,' he said, and she knew he meant Father Ben. 'I can't stop you. Even if I could I'd have no right to. But you've no idea how I'll worry about you. Manila's so dangerous, Dulce. Every day you read – but you know all that.'

'I'll be careful, Pecto, I promise. I don't want never to see you again, my family, my village, my friends.'

'But you can't go until after Flores de Mayo.'

'Of course not,' she laughed, thinking there was scarcely a season of the year when it *would* be timely to go, there was so much to be sung. Suddenly she had an insight into what she was leaving, the cultural orderliness of provincial life, and felt panic.

'Isn't it strange,' he said in his earnest way, speaking more to the horizon than to her. ' "I'm going to Manila", you said, and just four words make everything else unravel. If you hadn't said them everything might go on for ever like this.' He gazed at the beach, at the sea breaking aslant over the coral heads offshore as the tide wandered in. 'But now you've said them all sorts of other things feel overdue for ending. What will the choir be without you, Dulce? Your village? Even me?'

'You do exaggerate, Pecto,' she said fondly.

'Not by much. I don't mean I shall collapse, any more than the village, although the choir might. I mean suddenly we're all going to have to move on.'

'Theological college.'

'I don't know.'

'But you'll graduate from high school. Your grades are excellent.'

'It's not that.'

'No. What is it, Pecto? Really? You can tell me.'

But still he couldn't. They had walked up off the beach and across the narrow coastal road. Choir practice was in ten minutes. Dark was gathering among the palms. From a TV in someone's house came the introductory music of *Balitang Balita*, the six o'clock news. Naldo's doves were fluttering in to perch around their cote. For a moment one looked as though it were about to settle on Perfecto's serious young head and Dulce was reminded of a picture in the cathedral vestry which showed the Holy Ghost hovering above Christ, or maybe John the Baptist. It made her laugh.

'At least there's no brownout tonight. We can use the Yamaha keyboard instead of your guitar,' he said obliviously.

'No brownout *yet*,' she agreed, then impulsively squeezed his hand. 'Oh Pecto, I'm going to miss you. Let's make a pact before I go. I'll come back, I promise. Say two years.'

'No-one ever comes back,' he told her solemnly. 'If they do return it's as a different version, hadn't you noticed? Travel changes people. The precise person who leaves has left for ever. You and I will never see each other

again, you know. We'll be other people. "I'm going to
Manila." Four simple words, and everything changed for
ever.'

Yet sad though his delivery was, Dulce later thought he
hadn't really been speaking with her in mind. The weight
of his melancholy was already too well established, too
long since a part of him. As always, his words had an
obliqueness about them. Their accuracy was immediate
but their force came from elsewhere. Three months later
she was in Manila, her family having scraped together the
fare and a week's rent for Cousin Lita. A month after that
he replied to a brave, homesick letter from her with the
news that he was leaving home to join Father Ben, whose
absence had become unbearable. Perhaps because she was
now in the capital the clamp of provincial thinking was
eased and permitted her little mental leaps which made
new sense of old puzzles. She thought all the more fondly
of poor, troubled Pecto until it seemed that he, not she,
was truly lost and cut off from home.

Bambi Bar was only one of many in Pasay that had
benefited from the closure, by mayoral edict, of similar
dives in the traditional tourist area of Ermita. To its largely
local patrons were now added Australians and Pakistanis
and Germans who tended to come alone and sit for hours,
stunned by alcohol and made yet more torpid by the
air-con and battering of decibels. Gradually Dulce recognised one of them, a baldish pinkish man of maybe forty

(she wasn't good at judging foreigners' ages) whose round tub of belly pushed out a succession of gaudy Hawaiian shirts so their hems in front hung well clear of his belt when he stood up. She became aware of his attention, feeling his eyes fixed on her as she sang and seeing his hands applaud in the circle of light cast by the table lamp. A heavy gold signet ring gleamed up at her.

'*Ingat*,' said Rey the bouncer when he handed her a note as Dulce was snatching a rest in the dressing-room upstairs. 'Careful. If old Porky gives you trouble I can sort him out, don't you worry, Dulce. We stick together here.'

She smiled gratefully at Rey and opened the note. The foreigner was genuinely impressed by her act, thought her voice unique, had a business proposition to make her. She looked up but Rey had gone back on duty downstairs. She showed the note to Danny who was doing a little grass up on the roof.

'That's what they all say.' Danny handed it back. 'He just wants pussy. Take my word for it, kid. Just freeze him out.'

'But you don't know that,' she protested, unwilling to let a compliment fall so easily to dust.

'I would if I was him.' A cloud of fragrant smoke drifted off among the roof's rusty clutter. 'Joke only,' he added. 'But he's a man and so am I, and we men really only want one thing.'

'Is that so?' she cried, thinking of Perfecto and allowing herself the reassuring warmth of memory. What wouldn't she give to be home again at this moment! But what good would it do?

'Ah, come *on*, baby.' She noticed that the more he smoked the more he took on a fake Californian identity. 'You've been here six months now, right? There's only just so much mileage in being an innocent from the sticks. I mean you've got to swim with the tide.'

'Oh, you mean *you* would if it was you he was sending notes to?'

'Hell, no. There are tides and tides, sister. Got to be a bit choosy.'

But suddenly seeing him there, cross-legged on the mat in his stage gear and ponytail, she thought it probably wouldn't bother him at all, that there was nothing Danny mightn't do in his own interest. His heart was as involuted and insubstantial as smoke. *Plastik talaga.* She could see him as a faith healer or a hired killer, as the author of ingenious scams or as an eternal keyboard player in a lifetime of Bambi Bars.

'Just be careful of old Lettie,' he added. 'She doesn't take kindly to her girls messing with clients. She doesn't care about your virginity but she sure as hell cares if you're poached.'

Lettie Tan was Bambi Bar's owner, a powerful middle-aged Chinese *mestiza* with all the right connections in the underworld, police and judiciary to give her the required immunity to operate at a profit and do much else besides. Gossip said Lettie had her fingers in all sorts of pies, a scrubby bar in Pasay being so marginal to her real business interests it could only have been a convenient front for some racket or other; but Dulce had never wanted to know more. It was bad enough explaining to herself (let alone to her family back home) how it was that after half a year in this city she still wasn't the new Lea Salonga in a global smash hit which made *Miss Saigon* pale by comparison. She instinctively felt that the more she found out about her workplace, her employer and her fellow performers the further she would slide into their world and be unable to climb out. She decided to ignore the fat man's note, but he came again the next night and wrote her another which insisted that his motives were genuine.

'Sure they are,' Danny agreed when again she showed it him. 'Genuinely *malibog*.'

This vulgarity gave her the small shock required for another of her insights, which was that Danny might well be jealous. He wouldn't want to see her getting ahead, less because he would begrudge her success than because it would mean he was being left behind with the shades of Pasay closing in around him, condemned eternally to a world of strobe lighting, mud wrestling, beer fumes and *shabu* dealers. At a quarter to midnight, when her admirer was still sitting at his table, Dulce walked past him and smiled. Tired from two hours' singing, she stood on the pavement outside where the damp heat was strangely refreshing after the club's bacterial chill, the traffic noise reassuringly dull and vague after Danny's fortissimo pounding on the keyboard, the bludgeoning of the electronic drum-set. The pavements were still busy with people looking for a good time, a fruitless search which would occupy most of their three score years and ten but which the streets of Pasay appeared to suggest was at last within their grasp. Outside the doors of the various clubs stood blue-uniformed security men on a strip of stained carpet, often at a little desk with a ledger on it. They and the hostesses who came out for breathers would do their best to entice the passers-by inside, hospitably throwing open a door and releasing a waft of frigid air, a blast of music, a glimpse of shimmering ultra-violet costumes and flesh and suggestive darkness. Dulce couldn't imagine how the strollers made their choice; the clubs all offered much the same thing although each was tricked out with its own neon motif or gimmick, just as Bambi Bar girls were revealed by its opening door as wearing pert little scuts of nylon fur on their bottoms and not much else.

'I meant what I said.' The fat man was standing beside her, towering above her, mountainous. The crossed palm trees and orange suns printed on his shirt stretched to every horizon. The thing was the size of a tent, she thought irrelevantly. Imagine trying to wash that in the river. The others would die laughing, holding up their husbands' threadbare T-shirts beside it like so many handkerchiefs. 'Name's Carl.' His hand engulfed hers. 'I just had to see you. You've a fabulous voice, did you know that?' His accent was difficult for her; her own

English was mediocre. She became acutely conscious of her stage costume, knowing that to any passerby she would look like just another tart being picked up by some foreign slob. She smiled uncertainly and glanced at her watch. 'I know you can't talk now,' he said unexpectedly. 'I just wanted to ask if you were interested in a job down under.'

'Down under?'

'Sydney,' Carl explained. 'My home town. Okay – don't answer now. Just are you interested, in principle?' She nodded. 'In that case I'll give you my card. When's your day off? When are you free?'

'Wednesday afternoon,' she said, thinking of her only day for catching up on the sleep she seemed to need more and more. 'Sometimes.'

'Okay. I'll be in the Midtown Ramada, Room 207, this Wednesday afternoon. Come if you can. Come if you want. But I'm flying out again Friday. It's up to you . . . I didn't get your name? Dulce? Pretty. Stage or real? Not that it matters. Okay, then.'

He lumbered away, heaping a jowl on to one shoulder as he looked back for a passing cab and leaving her holding a card whose embossed lettering (she ran an impressed finger over it) announced him as Carl Spanier of Spanier Entertainments (Pty), Sydney.

All this was so evidently a dream her impulse was to keep it to herself. Otherwise she would feel such a fool when it didn't come true. But at last she did tell Danny, pointing out a little defiantly that this was the sort of businessman who had embossed cards and stayed at the best hotels, not some fast-talking scumbag living in one of those pension houses or motels which charged two-hourly rates. But all Danny would do was jerk his head in acquiescence and echo Rey's '*Ingat*'. 'Take care, that's all.'

When she awoke on Wednesday midday in her ply-wood cubicle she washed and dressed attentively, even pilfering a squirt or two of young Lerma's 'Frenzy' before eating a nervous lunch of rice and broth and catching a jeepney to the Midtown Ramada. This, she thought as she crossed a gleaming marble floor dotted with shrubs, liveried bell-boys and knots of foreigners gathered around heaps of expensive luggage, was the first step in what would surely become her natural habitat as an international singer. She wondered if she could pinch some of the hotel's headed stationery on which to write home. Dulce didn't know whether to feel disappointment or relief when, having announced her on the house phone, the receptionist said that Mr Spanier would come down to meet her in the Coffee Shop in five minutes.

She went through, was shown a table and glanced through the menu, hoping her amazement at the prices wouldn't be noticed by her neighbours and betray her as a girl fresh from the provinces. But really – a pot of chocolate would set you back nearly half what she earned for a hard night's singing. At that moment Carl came up with a Filipino in his twenties who had the sort of matinée idol hairstyle that ex-President Marcos had affected, a gleaming, Presleyesque sweep. Evidently Carl dressed conservatively during daylight hours; he was wearing dark slacks and a plain white shirt whose hem still overhung his belt like the valance of a curtain. He introduced his companion as Boy Torres, who took her hand with a knowing wink. Carl, by contrast, was polite and slightly formal as if he repented his night-time persona.

'Glad you could make it,' he said. 'Now, have you ordered? No? Should have. What'll you have?'

'I'd like a pot of chocolate,' Dulce said, with what she hoped was the right amount of casualness.

While they were waiting she caught Boy's complicitous glances which seemed to say 'I know you, babe. I know your miserable village and I know your schoolgirl dreams. I know where you're at. You and me, we understand each other. Tagalog? Ilokano? Cebuano? I don't care what your language is, I speak it too. The only foreigner here's old Fatso. I'm on your side. We'll work something out.' And again the wink.

Three pots of chocolate arrived and were served into white cups like dollops of fragrant mud.

'I was telling Boy here about your lovely voice,' Carl said, 'and he can't wait to hear you. Boy's my agent here in Manila, my business associate, I guess you'd say. He scouts the talent for me when I'm not around. What I do, I run an entertainments agency. Solo singers, dancers, pop groups, live acts, circus acts, magic shows, you name it.

But only the best. You're in the right place, you know.
Forget the Old World. South-east Asia, the Pacific Rim,
Australasia: this is where the action is now. The real
money, the real economic future's right here. People all
over from Korea to Tasmania want the best and by God
they can pay for it. I only deal in the best, right, Boy? He'll
tell you. I don't care about the rest. They can go off and
play hick towns in the States or do yawny-porny cabarets
in Manchester and Hamburg. Let 'em go. Only the best
for Spanier Entertainments and from what I've listened to
these last few nights you're the best. Or you easily could
be, with a bit of proper training. How old are you, Dulce?'

'Eighteen.'

'Is that true?' Boy asked her in Tagalog. 'No point in
lying. You'll need a birth certificate for your passport
application.'

'It's true,' she said in English.

'You look younger,' Carl said appreciatively, 'but that's
advantageous. Ever had any voice training?'

Dulce thought she couldn't recall a time when she hadn't
been singing. The school concerts, the choirs, the Flores de
Mayo . . . 'Well,' she said, 'not really. Lack of funds.'

'I thought so, but we can arrange that easily enough.
Read music?'

'Oh yes,' she said, thinking of the tonic sol-fa hymn
sheets with the numbered guitar chords.

'That's great. Pretty rare, too. You're one in a
thousand, believe me. Education?'

'High school graduate,' she said proudly.

'Wow. I'm beginning to think you're overqualified,' he said and then, catching sight of her look of dismay, added 'Only kidding. You need brains to get ahead, sing well, pick up a new act. We've enough Kleenex-brains in the industry as it is. You married, Dulce?'

'No,' she said, knowing she was blushing.

'Not even nearly?'

'No.' How did one answer a question like that, especially when asked by a complete stranger? What was nearly? And if one said no, how was it possible to counter a faint suggestion that one was slow in love, nearly out of one's teens with chances slipping by? Or else a bit fast, not to say downright loose?

'What I mean,' explained Carl, 'is you'd be completely free to take up a job abroad if one came up? No family encumbrances, clinging boyfriends, emotional complications, that sort of thing?'

'Nothing like that.' From the corner of her eye she could glimpse Boy staring at her.

'Fine. Tell me, Dulce, what do you want? I mean, in the best of all worlds what would you like to be?'

How different he was from Perfecto, she thought; how strange that an earnest young boy and this pink middle-aged Australian should ask her the same question. Where did their interests coincide? She was amazed to hear herself giving Pecto's own answer.

'Truthfulness.'

'How's that again?'

'I mean,' she said hurriedly, 'I want to be myself. All I am is a singer. I want to be a singer. I really love music, you see.' And in case this sounded too feebly self-indulgent she added 'To earn a living, I mean. I guess I'm ambitious.' She took a decisive swig of the chocolate which even felt like sweet mud in her mouth it was so thick and rich, falling down her gullet like silt.

'I reckon that's pretty much what I wanted to hear.' Carl sat back with an encouraging smile. 'You've no idea the number of kids I talk to, young wannabes of every kind. Singers, keyboard players, guitar-bashers, percussion nerds. The one thing most of them never say – never even *hint* at – is that they love what they do. That's why the majority of them will never make it. Not in a million years. You can't hope to make a profession out of music without, first and foremost, a love of music. It comes even before talent and a long, long way before skill. Skills can be taught, love can't. Am I right?'

'Oh yes!' she cried, at last warming to this odd blowsy businessman with the voluminous shirts and the Dunhill watch whose crocodile strap was sunk deep in fat and hair. Wasn't this what she'd always said to Lisel and Marivic and all those other know-all schoolfriends of hers who yearned only to get up on a stage, never mind what they'd do once they'd got there? 'I know that's right!'

It felt like a real intimacy between them, which made it all the more disconcerting when Carl looked at his watch and said 'Hey, Dulcie, I've got to dash. As I said, I'm flying out to Oz day after tomorrow, got a million things to do before then. Do you mind if I leave you and Boy to complete the formalities? I assume you haven't got a passport so we'll have to start the ball rolling. Don't worry about it – Boy's got fixers all lined up who'll take care of the whole thing.' He pushed back his chair.

'But,' said Dulce, 'I mean, thanks for the chocolate, Mr Spanier.'

'Carl, for Pete's sake. Where d'you get this Mr Spanier stuff? If you're coming to Oz you'll have to loosen up and get pally, Dulcie.'

'What I mean is, Carl, have I got a job? Am I really going to Australia?'

But Carl would only say 'Speak to the man. Bye, Dulcie', and waddled off through the Coffee Shop calling 'Spanier, two-o-seven, right?' to their waitress.

'*Tará*,' said Boy.

'Where to?'

'The office.'

They took a taxi to a block of apartments two streets over from Roxas Boulevard, not far from Malate Church. The lift wasn't working. Apprehensively Dulce followed the heels of Boy's white sneakers as they climbed two flights to an unmarked door.

– You've got to be kidding – her Guardian Angel said faintly, but all she could hear was the sound of her own best shoes on the gritty cement. She was only partially relieved to see that the main room was indeed set up as an office although there wasn't a secretary in sight.

'Relax. Sit down.' He pushed a button on a cassette deck and the room filled with the sound of Charlene singing 'I've never been to me'. It was one of Dulce's favourite songs and she couldn't help humming along with it. 'How about a drink?'

'I don't drink, thanks.'

'Kalamansi juice? Coke?'

'A cold kalamansi would be nice,' she admitted. Its acid, citrus bite would hopefully cut through the last of the chocolate which still seemed to be coating her teeth and tongue. Boy Torres disappeared. There came the distant sound of a refrigerator door, clinking glasses, stirring.

> 'I've no doubt
> you dream about
> the things you never do;
> but I wish someone
> had talked to me
> like I wanna talk to you,'

sang Charlene warningly, winding up to her world-weary discovery that paradise was a lie. Then Boy came back with two glasses.

– Basically – her Guardian Angel announced inaudibly – you're on your own. –

'See, I'm having one too,' said Boy. 'I left the spoon in

yours in case you wanted more sugar. Okay, now.' He sat behind the large desk and messed about with sheets of paper, finally straightening some up in front of him and picking up a pen. 'Names? Date of birth?'

She gave the answers obediently in between sips of the juice which was delightfully cold in her mouth.

'Place of occupation – yuh, Bambi Bar, 2361 Santiago, Pasay.'

'How did you know that?' she asked in surprise.

He gave her an impatient glance. 'How do you think? Carl went there three nights running, didn't he?'

Of course. Yes, how stupid of her. She was finding it hard to concentrate because of the music. It was always the same with her: if people talked against music it was the music which took her attention, no matter how important the conversation. She had the urge to kick off her shoes and sing, really let herself go. But the chair was comfortable and she was content to sit there for as long as he liked, answering silly questions about herself, her home address, her next of kin. Why couldn't these documents say 'family'? 'Next of kin' sounded so ominous, more like drawing up a will than applying for a fabulous future.

Boy Torres was looking at her. He patted his quiff. 'Give us a song, then, Dulce. Go on, sing along. I've never heard you.' He crossed to the cassette deck and rewound the tape. 'I've never been to me' started again.

Dulce put down her empty glass and heard the music

pounding within her as if it were welling up from an internal source, so fresh and urgent it sounded. With sudden abandon she lay back in her chair and began belting it out fit to fill an auditorium:

'I've been
undressed by kings
and I've seen some things
that a woman ain't s'posed to see;
I've been to paradise
but I've never been to me'

only it didn't come belting out but emerged as a faint, little girl's wailing which surprised her very much. Boy Torres merely smiled a bit more.

'Are you a virgin, Dulce?'

'I don't believe that's in the questionnaire,' she squeaked severely.

'We have a need to know,' he said, putting down his ballpen and coming around the desk.

– I really will be off now, – her Guardian Angel told her faintly. – I clean forgot about drugs. Look, I'm really sorry. I goofed. What can I say? –

This time she was hearing her Angel's words but they were so slow she began to lose their meaning. She did notice they fitted exactly to the music, that in fact Charlene was singing the words as he spoke them. She was lying on a bed, it seemed, and a small, slippery sensation which had been going on for some time now began spreading an urgent warmth through her. She thought of Perfecto but perversely it was Carl Spanier's huge face swimming in front of her accompanied by a crushing sensation which was not at all disagreeable. Carl promptly melted into Boy Torres. Handsome brute, she thought, and Pecto's earnest entreaties drifted away. The desire which replaced them was probably unassuageable.

When Dulce awoke the room was dark. There was a man lying beside her. She was ragingly thirsty. She stumbled about the apartment, turning on lights until she found the kitchen and drank four glasses of water straight off. Her legs were weak and felt cold. Looking down, she discovered she was naked below the waist. She pulled her blouse together at her throat and the gesture made her aware of her desolation.

'You bastard,' she said as Boy came in, fully clothed.

'Huh? Is that a nice way to greet your lover, Dulce?'

'*Lover*? Rapist, more like.'

'Oh sure, some rapist. You were fabulous, kid. I've never known anyone put out like that. Talk about hot to trot. I'm exhausted.'

Disgusted and humiliated she leaned against the sink and wept quietly.

'You don't believe me?' he asked her. 'Look at your legs. Go look at the bed. See any blood? Torn clothes? Do I look as if I had to fight my way in?'

'Drugs,' she said bitterly. 'You drugged me.'

But there was no proof, no-one she could turn to who mightn't have tangled her in still worse trouble. Boy Torres, like Lettie Tan, undoubtedly had good connections; you needed them in the recruitment business. Go to the police with a hoary old story like hers and she'd be asking to get squashed, maybe even terminally. With reckless extravagance she took a cab back to her lodgings, head pounding and heart sick. It was eleven-thirty at night. Even before washing she phoned the Ramada to be told that Mr Spanier was not in his room. The next morning when she woke at ten it appeared Mr Spanier had already checked out.

'Checked out? But it's only Thursday.' She thought for a long moment in which the busy receptionist, evidently thinking there was no more to be said, broke the connection.

The scattered wisps of her recollection acquired the weightlessness of a dream, too insubstantial to be allowed to interfere with her professional future. After all, she might well have imagined the fat man's presence in the office; the sole reality was having woken in a bed beside Boy. She therefore wrote Carl a dignified, guarded letter asking him whether she might apply to him direct since his Manila agent, Mr Torres, had revealed himself to be a person with whom no single girl would wish to do business. The weeks of waiting for his reply stretched themselves out. In this time Dulce rehearsed every kind of hopelessness and remorse. She simply had to go abroad now. She didn't want to stay a day longer than necessary in this city and there was no way she could go home. That was what she longed for, of course: to return to her family but not as a failure and a disgrace. No money, no career, no father for the baby which even now might be taking shape inside her, a contaminating mannikin with a miniature quiff of hair . . . For the same reason she couldn't even run back to Cousin Lita in Parañaque. Her fellow-boarders became alarmed by her sudden tearfulness. One day on the radio she heard somebody singing 'Amazing Grace', which had been one of her own best-loved and most often requested numbers in the choir back home. It broke her up completely. They carried her to her cubicle and drew the curtain and two of the girls sat with her and did each other's nails as Dulce cried herself to sleep. Privy to her secret, they were horrified and phlegmatic. That was the way things were.

But they weren't privy to her most terrible secret of all, the one which truly left her life in ruins. For Dulce had lost her voice. Oh, she could still sing, but it wasn't the same. She found she could no longer throw back her head and let the soul flood out of her mouth as before. She still had the notes, the words, the skill; but something had died, maybe even music itself. Her firm belief became that she would only ever regain her true voice by going abroad. Surely in Sydney or Hong Kong or Tokyo it would at once return in its former glory. As long as she stayed here, though, she

would be a mere performer instead of a real musician. This
defection, this desertion by her most intimate faculty
caused her the greatest anguish of all.

Her position at Bambi Bar had changed, too. Lettie Tan
had greeted her coldly when she checked in for work that
Thursday afternoon.

'We don't take kindly to traitors here,' she said.

'What do you mean, Ma'am?' Dulce asked. 'Who have I
betrayed?'

'You know perfectly well what I mean. It may be your
idea of loyalty to an employer to spend your afternoon off
lounging around the Midtown Ramada in the company of
notorious illegal recruiters, but it's not mine.'

Dulce had been so shocked to find that Lettie knew,
she'd been unable to say a word. Lettie had further reduced
her already meagre pay to that of a hostess since it 'was
clearly more appropriate'. That night Dulce had done her
best to sing but the previous day's events and the sight of
her employer lurking in the freezing shadows, sourly
scanning the few customers and the lacklustre act, turned
everything into a nightmare. She forgot words, she
missed cues, she couldn't find her heart. Every so often
she'd catch sight of Danny's face, a mask of gnomic
indifference lit from below by his keyboard's white plastic
glare. Only later did she work out that it must have been
he who'd shopped her to Lettie. Only he had known
where she was going. And yet . . . Dulce could never be
absolutely certain. One never knew the full extent of these

people's power, the network of their informers, the tabs they kept.

One day nearly a month after she had written to Australia an envelope arrived. Dulce tore it open and read that Spanier Entertainments (Pty) thanked her for her letter but regretted that Mr Carl Spanier had been deceased for nine years. Consequently any business undertaken by a person purporting to be him had no legal validity whatever.

I don't *know* about you, Danny, she thought exhaustedly at him as she lay between acts on the mat on Bambi Bar's roof that night. I don't know about anyone any more. I don't even know about myself. The keyboard player was outlined against the night sky, leaning over the coping, smoke lazing up around his ponytail, gazing down into the street far below with eyes which glittered with neon. She ached and ached for home, for her brother Noriel and the rest of her family, for the beach at dusk with the sea quietly rinsing the strand, for the fireflies and choir practices and the haunting old hymns and songs. But it was impossible. Such shame; such betrayal. A tear slipped down her cheek, cutting a trail through the rouge and powder she hated to wear.

Later that night – or it might have been on another occasion around that desolate time – Danny, whose laconic, knowing antennae must have been quivering and dabbing like those of a cockroach, said that now she'd got used to life without her virginity might she not fancy a bit occasionally? Like now would do fine, he suggested. Right here on this very mat. Much more refreshing than sleep. Light up a toke, chill out.

'We're none of us virgins in this life,' he volunteered with surprising regret in his voice, and let a not un-sympathetic silence develop for a minute or two while the cacophony of midnight revelry, bar music and traffic shuddered up from below. 'I'm even a little envious,' he added. 'Me, I've got nothing except my keyboard. At least you can become a whore.' But he used a beautiful and forgiving Tagalog euphemism, '*kalapating mababa ang lipad*', a low-flying dove.

People's Disgrace

FROM BOYHOOD ON, Feodor Sarin had been fascinated by codes, ciphers and numerologies of all kinds. That he had an extraordinary head for figures was recognised by his schoolmates, particularly those who shared his passion for train-spotting. A serious-faced, peaky lad in spectacles, bundled up to twice his size against the cold, he would stand for hours at the ends of platforms. Unlike the others, though, Feodor carried no notebook and pencil. He could memorise any engine's number at a glance and – though this had yet to be thoroughly tested – recall it perfectly years later. And that was only half his talent. He could also remember the precise pitch of a whistle so that, as the boys ran down to the station when school was out and heard the sharp toot of an engine about to leave, Feodor would shout:

'That's two-o-seven-seven-three-one-two-one. *Zhaporets* class. Betcha. Anything you like!'

He was always right, which didn't make him any more popular but which confirmed him in a class of his own and on his own – one of those freakish kids whose talent is so weird, so spectacularly futile, that at most it only ever earns an awed contempt. In winter when the long-haul trains pulled in on their journey from the dark landscapes of the far north, little Feodor would be there on the platform in the snow flurries, gazing seriously at the ginger fangs of frozen urine caked beneath the ends of the carriages, the blocks of excrement moulded by wind into fantastic streamlined sculptures, hundredweights of stained incrustation set like iron and waiting for the steam hoses in Central Station four hundred miles away. The huge locomotives which hauled these trains cried a mournful three-note chord: a deep minor triad which wailed away across the wastes as though the engines were expressing the endless melancholy of the steppe and forest through which they passed. At night Feodor heard the sound in bed and his eyes would fill with involuntary tears: something to do with being able to identify the particular engine, with being able to follow an old friend out of the station and away on its unseen trajectory; with distance and loss.

As time went by Feodor's teachers found themselves forced to make difficult distinctions about him. Either he was greatly talented and quite without gifts or he was hugely gifted and utterly without talent. 'He has an ear for mathematics,' succinctly observed Dr Ugarev. 'Come to that,' said Dr Rubinskaya, who taught Feodor the piano, 'he has a head for music.' 'But no heart, eh?' 'Who knows?' Rubinskaya asked. 'We've only the school doctor's word for it that Feodor *has* a heart. I freely confess the boy's a complete enigma to me.'

Whether it was talent or gift he lacked Feodor undoubtedly had a bent for music, for it increasingly inclined his adolescence towards musical studies at university. Without it he might have turned into one of those obsessive youths who slowly vanish into themselves before surfacing again in their early twenties to announce with calm, crazed intensity that the future can be predicted from the precise position of the name 'Jehovah' in the Bible, from the dimensions of the Great Pyramid, or from the relative masses and periodicity of the inner planets. Instead, he went to study music at the prestigious Academy at Mekanograd. Feodor proved to have a heart after all, for here he met and fell in love with Nicolai Ghiaurov. Oh, *he* didn't know it was love; whatever signs of romance or the erotic in Feodor's life were far too obscure for so commonplace a diagnosis. Until then he had only ever come close to expressing any such thing in a poem written at fifteen, when he'd vaguely had at the back of his mind the presence of a fellow train-spotter, a boy named Basil with sticking-out ears. It had been a prodigious intellectual exercise in which Feodor had set himself the challenge of writing a sonnet in code in which both coded and decoded versions preserved the correct rhyme scheme. *En clair*, it was entitled 'Pistons at Dawn'; and although it did make syntactical sense in both versions even the poet had to concede that much meaning was not readily apparent in either. None the less, it seemed to him to tremble on the edge of intelligibility in a most tantalising and profound way. He certainly never showed it to Basil, whom in any case he despised for being dim-witted.

This Ghiaurov, by contrast, was unquestionably talented as a composer. He was short and beautiful and carried everywhere with him a gun-metal pencil case like those used by rural doctors for their clinical thermometers. Whenever an idea struck him he would pull the little cylinder's cap off with a hermetic *pop!* and take out a freshly sharpened pencil, releasing with it the resinous smell of cedar. With this he would scribble notes on the back of an envelope or on the flyleaf of a book. Feodor Sarin watched, fascinated.

'You, of course, could remember without having to write it down, little Einstein of the tundra?'

'Well, yes, I could.'

'Only tell me how and I shall be your friend for life.'

'I don't know,' his devoted admirer admitted. 'I guess I turn the notes into digits. Yes, I'm pretty sure I do. It's so quick I never have to think, you see. I don't imagine I could remember tunes on their own. They can't exist by themselves.'

'So in your bizarre world Beethoven's Fifth starts "5–5–5–3; 4–4–4–2"?'

'It's not as crude as that!' cried Feodor. 'You have to take the note-values into account, establish the key, the time,

all sorts of things. Just numbering all the notes of the
octave one to eight or even one to thirteen would be no
more than the dumbest substitution cipher. But I can't
really say because I've never really thought about it. It's
like . . . like when I see you come into the lecture theatre
and I smell cedar and think "Nicolai!" but I don't have to
think "N-I-C-".'

'Do you know, no-one here knows if you're a genius or
a freak.'

'That,' Feodor said with startling dignity, 'is their
problem. To me, I'm me.'

'And what music does "N-I-C-" conjure up?'

'It's the sound the Azovskiy Express makes in summer
when its air horns are already hot with the sun. Loco
number seven-five-double-o-nine-nine-eight-one. It's a
true D flat rather than the C sharp it has in winter. You can
tell the day's temperature from a locomotive's sound.
Coefficient of expansion. Simple physics. Your name is
summer for me.'

Thereafter young Ghiaurov never laughed at Feodor,
never again called him the Einstein of the tundra or
blinked birdily with the other students in imitation of his
spectacled gaze. In fact he became quite protective and, if
the truth be known, awed by a strangeness of mind which
he was powerless to evaluate. For his own part Feodor
enviously adored Ghiaurov's straightforward musicianship, his ability to improvise at the piano and invent
hummable tunes.

It was inevitable, therefore, that Feodor Sarin should have gravitated towards the purely academic discipline of musicology. His doctoral thesis was on music and encryption, whose roots he laboriously traced to the fifteenth-century Burgundian and Flemish schools, to the parody masses of such composers as Binchois and Josquin. He obtained (and even more laboriously read, since his English was not good) articles by the British musicologist Eric Sams who proposed that Schumann had used cipher extensively in his music. Sams had 'decoded' all sorts of words and phrases. Feodor was interested to discover that when similar methods were applied to other extracts and, indeed, to other composers, a variety of messages floated to the surface. In one of his cantatas Bach appeared to be groaning in German (even as his tenor bewailed the weight of sin dragging him down) 'Six thalers a pound is coffee tod.' It was tempting to invent the two extra notes needed to complete 'today' (if that was what it was) but try as he might Feodor couldn't juggle them right. Still, the bulk of the 'decoded' sentence seemed perfectly intelligible, though he did wonder why Bach should have bothered to make the remark at all. The same went for a phrase in Haydn's *Creation* where the violas said 'Dislike all mountains, O.' More scandalously, Chopin in one of his scherzos confessed 'I long to suck his toenails' in French. Using a complex series of probability curves Feodor eventually worked out what commonsense had already told him, which was that any coherent notation system – whether of notes, letters, digits or symbols – could, by applying selective rules, be made to yield almost any 'concealed' text. But doing the research and putting it all together as a thesis was stimulating and rewarded him with Mekanograd's most brilliant doctorate in years.

All this happened as great events were shaking the country. He might have spent his first twenty years in a world of his own, wrapped in steam, but Feodor was perfectly aware that he'd done so in revolutionary times. There was little one couldn't gather by simply standing at the ends of platforms in an obscure provincial railway station. Troop trains, hospital trains; goods trains consisting of nothing but bulk cement wagons or steel girders; the fluctuations of passenger expresses on their seasonal pilgrimage to the southern coasts; all these could be read. But now came the denunciations. They hadn't been revolutionary times at all, apparently, merely *revisionist*. The original ideals had been betrayed; a flabbiness had been allowed to creep in because the leaders themselves had hankerings for the *ancien régime*. They did their shopping in exclusive stores full of imported luxuries; their bedrooms were scented and had libraries of pornographic videos.

Feodor had bidden a sad goodbye to his only friend Nicolai, whose own postgraduate years had been spent giving lessons in composition, and went home with his newly minted doctorate to visit his parents. He had barely arrived when a buff envelope with a revolutionary slogan

printed across its flap reached him. The letter it contained
was from the Academicians' Union and urged him to
report at once for vital patriotic service in the capital. An
ancient *Lubomir* class loco he'd never seen before hauled
him slowly thither while he stared at the sliding landscape
through spectacle lens and dusty pane, reflecting that since
Lubomirs were essentially a sixty-year-old short-haul
design it must mean the big *Khans* and *Zhaporets* had been
diverted to more pressing tasks than chuffing musicologists about the country. He couldn't imagine why the
Union had sent for him; but on reaching the unsmiling
granite edifice he was soon informed that he'd been chosen
from a thousand possible candidates to head the newly
formed Board of Musical Purity.

'The what?' he asked. The concept rang no bells.

'Essentially, and by any other name, you're the music
censor,' he was told. 'Our comrades in the Art Theory
department have convincingly shown how wrong we've
been until now in allowing our native composers to
become contaminated by foreign decadence. In short,
we're at last taking seriously the example our great
neighbour the USSR has been setting in condemning all
that decadent Jewish cacophony by Schoenberg and others
of the Second Viennese School. Music's no different from
any other art: it must be firmly anchored in social
relevance otherwise it leads inevitably to the effete cult of
the individual moaning on about his own precious sensibility and mortality. What ordinary person ever whistled

twelve-tone music as he worked? Your own region is, of course, particularly rich in characteristic folk music.'

'It is?' asked Feodor. He tried to recall the tonal landscape of his native province but could hear only the whistles and hooters and sirens of railway engines.

'Yes, they told us you were a wag.' A clap on the back and a guffaw. 'This is your office. Basically, you have a staff of ten. All the music publishers are bound to submit any new composition to your department first for checking. Your people will be testing it for social relevance, which is comparatively easy. The reason we picked *you* is because of your ability to spot the subtler kinds of counter-revolutionary thought, even deliberate sabotage. We read your thesis, you know. Quite brilliant. We realised at once that you're the only person who could possibly do this vital cultural job. That's why your salary's unusually high.'

And so at the age of twenty-four Feodor Sarin became willy-nilly the country's chief music censor. He soon found the work was pretty dull and routine. Daily his subordinates waded through new submissions; and while at first they threw out nearly everything, the changed climate soon began to make itself felt. Compositions began arriving with titles like 'A Popular Symphony'; 'Quintet – The Land Reform'; and, in the case of a triumphal cantata for peasant voices, 'Fowl Pest Eradicated Through Correct Thought'. Feodor might not have been a wag but neither was he stupid. He subjected the

Fowl Pest cantata to a personal scrutiny for hidden expressions of discontent. For one electrifying moment he thought he'd found treason in the brass section during the farmer's anguished outcry at the silence which has suddenly fallen over his poultry sheds. 'Balls to the Motherland' seemed to be the *cantus firmus* before Feodor pulled himself together and realised it was nothing of the kind. These were transposing instruments, in any case. He was thankful he hadn't told anyone before double-checking. The fact was that under enough pressure of duty and expectation a musical text could take on the attributes of a Rorschach ink blot. Stare at it long enough and you could read unsettling things which could only have one source . . . Besides, every cryptography scholar had taken to heart the awful example of the New York lawyer, James Martin Feely, who in 1943 had entered the lists of the great Roger Bacon controversy by publishing a 'solution' to part of the manuscript which read, famously: 'The feminated, having been feminated, press on the forebound; those pressing on are moistened; they are veinladen; they will be broken up; they are lessened.' It might as well be the ineffable Nostradamus as medieval proctology.

Feodor soon made another discovery, which was that his salary was unusually paltry. On the other hand the job for some reason included a good deal of free travel so he was able to slip away from the capital to attend music festivals in distant provinces. The festivals were a bore but

there was lots to drink and opportunities for spotting fresh
locos. He began to earn the reputation of being a first-rate
Party man. Then without warning the most dreadful
event of his life began taking shape, although for a time
it was completely unrecognisable. A competition was
announced for a new National Anthem. The old one, the
ideologues had decided, was too identified with the
revisionist era. The tune was too bland, the words too
self-consciously literary (the first two lines ran: 'The
Morning Star at early dawn/Is the Motherland's unsleep-
ing eye'). First some new words had to be written and
approved, and then they had to be set to an appropriate
tune. Some months went by until the Academy decided it
could accept a poem beginning 'From the Subiy to the
Plaszhda,/From the Borin to the Bob' and the nation's
composers were asked to submit suitable music under a
system which guaranteed anonymity until a firm choice
was made. In this way, it was felt, no Academician would
be swayed by an illustrious name to endorse an indifferent
tune.

While this was going on Feodor found himself con-
sidering national anthems in general. Most were remark-
ably bad. The new words just chosen were merely another
instance of the time-honoured trope of setting the
country's physical limits by reference to mountain ranges
and rivers. He did some research in the library. Brazilians
had their Ypiranga River in the first line; the Germans the
Maas, the Memel, the Etsch and the Belt in their opening

verse. Practically all without exception contained references to freedom, victorious armies, shining purpose and so forth, like the closing scene at the end of a Hollywood movie. That was what they mostly had in common, Feodor decided. They were expressions of happy endings. The country was like a rock; its leaders were unshakable; its people contented. A glorious future of something-or-other could henceforth eternally unfurl beneath the banners of whatever-it-was. No mention was anywhere made of rotten monarchs, low-life dictators, vile presidents, abject poverty, lost wars, one-sided trade pacts, border disputes or murderous ethnic divisions. Meanwhile, what of the music? 'All national anthems are still diatonic', he read in Grove's *Dictionary*. Was that right? he wondered. He looked at the front of the volume: 1954. Probably that had been correct then, but now? What did we know of the North Korean national anthem? Or that of Laos? If the Afghani national anthem (say) was diatonic would it be in response to some unwritten international pressure to conform to Western standards of singability? Did the conventions of Olympic Games demand that winning teams be heralded with recognisable tunes? Was this another triumph for cultural imperialism or was the Academy right after all, and people didn't intentionally whistle atonally while they worked?

One morning he found a large envelope on his desk. It contained a sheet of music MS and a note from the President of the National Anthem Co-ordinating

Committee saying that this had been unanimously judged
the winning entry, but before the composer's name could
be revealed the tune should – according to law – first be
submitted to Comrade Sarin's expert scrutiny since any
afterthought would be *more than embarrassing*. Feodor took
this to mean that a mistake on his part could well prove
fatal. The intensification of 'state discipline' had, of all new
measures, been the most enthusiastically pursued. With
this in mind he cleared his desk, unhooked his telephone,
locked the door and got down to work, prepared to sniff
out the least hint of a musical quotation from the old
Emperor's Hymn.

He soon saw it was quite a good tune. It was rousing,
but saved from the banality of its kind by a certain acidity
in the Prokofiev manner. Being scored in simple four-part
harmony it covered half a side of paper. At first he detected
nothing amiss; then on staring out of the window and
replaying one of the phrases in his head he ran it
backwards. Still nothing; yet . . . Like Bach himself, or
any of the great contrapuntists, he was incapable of
hearing a simple phrase without simultaneously being
aware of its possibilities in different topological guises:
cancrizans, inversion, diminution and augmentation,
major and minor . . . At last he found it, the evidence of
treason. It wasn't even very well concealed. Not that
anyone else could have spotted it, of course. Feodor sat
back so relieved and pleased with himself that he was
inclined to be over-generous to the poor fool who'd hoped

to get away with it. The give-away had been the recurrence of a five-note phrase. It appeared in the tenor part at the end of the halfway cadence and re-appeared in the alto part (with very slight modification) at the end of the entire tune. Since hymn cadences very often do repeat themselves it was unobtrusive, but to the truly expert ear and eye there could be no question as to the composer's intentions. A straightforward algorithm underlay the letter-for-note substitution. Decoded, the message halfway was 'Hi Mom!' and at the end 'Hi Pop!'

Feodor smiled as he vigorously polished his glasses. This was better than tracking down popular *chansons* embedded backwards in fifteenth-century masses. Surely saving the Republic from international ribaldry and humiliation at least deserved a rise in salary? He ringed the offending phrases in red, wrote a covering note explaining the trick and the preciseness of its solution, and sent it all back to the National Anthem Co-ordinating Committee feeling that at last he'd done something to justify a seemingly useless talent. The next thing he knew was that he was summoned by the President of the Academy to receive a commendation and a personal handshake. On the way out he was also given a stern warning by an aide that this whole affair was never to be spoken of again. If it ever leaked out, this man hinted, it would be understood to have come from *only one source*. Suitably cowed, Feodor said his lips were sealed for ever. That was a good thing, the aide told him, because the composer of this piece of heinous subversion was known to have been a friend of his and no-one wanted to have to make accusations of conspiracy, not unless they had to.

'But I've no idea who the composer is!' Feodor protested in alarm. 'The manuscript was pseudonymous.'

'We know that. But we also have the key to all the entrants. He's your old friend Nicolai Ghiaurov.'

'*Nicolai!*'

It spoke well of Feodor and of his genuine love that he was far more grief stricken at having unwittingly exposed his friend's prank than he was scared of being compromised by association. Only later, in the self-inquisitorial small hours, did the terrible likelihood strike him. *There was no treason.* There was only his own misplaced zeal, his resourceful genius for manipulating the innocent until it yielded the furtive. Now all he could think was how he could get in touch with poor Nicolai and apologise. How could he explain that he'd truly had no idea who'd written the tune? And so began his long anguish, that worst of all injustices when dear friends are separately led to believe that one has betrayed the other and neither is allowed redress: no explanation, no excuse, no contact. For the first time he learned the huge weight of cruelty at the disposal of those who cared for nothing. Feodor knew without asking that any attempt to trace his friend would lead not to Nicolai but to his own arrest. He thought of the balsamic scent of freshly whittled cedar which flooded out of his friend's pencil case when it was uncapped. He saw

Nicolai standing in a patch of sunlight with his books under one arm drawing a dotted crotchet in the gravel with the toe of one shoe to illustrate a point and heard again the sound of summer, a chord of D flat as though the Azovskiy Express were passing somewhere in the distance beyond immeasurable wheatfields. He wept, knowing he would never see Nicolai again. He was wrong.

A month or two went by and one day it was announced that there was to be a People's Disgrace on Saturday morning at nine. This was a form of punishment recently introduced for those guilty of the very worst crimes such as treason. It was one thing to have show trials but another to hold show punishments. They were very effective provided they were not so frequent as to inspire indifference. The new revolutionary authorities had to take into account several such considerations. If the direst punishments became mere commonplace spectacles they would not only lose their force but might even have the reverse effect of inspiring sympathy for the victims, on the grounds that they couldn't all be guilty of heinous crimes. And if they *were* all guilty, that would suggest widespread opposition to the government. There again, constant exposure to casual barbarity had inured most people to the threat of exemplary torture. Indeed, centuries of cruelty had staled them to everything but cynical humour. In a moment of inspiration someone had hit on the idea of combining execution with ridicule: the awe-inspiring People's Disgrace. This took place in public in the capital

– specifically on the Promena, a leafy boulevard overlooking a bend in the River Bob. There, against a patriotic
backdrop of the domes, towers and minarets of the eastern
city on the distant bank, the people would visit terminal
disgrace upon a national enemy.

To his horror Feodor found he was obliged to attend.
All government departments had to be represented. The
salutary effects of a People's Disgrace would be severely
limited if the only witnesses were the masses. Not until he
tremblingly took his seat on the hastily erected stand
facing the river did he and his colleagues learn the victim's
name and crime. In huge red letters on a white banner
the message wavered in the early breeze. NICOLAI
GHIAUROV: NATIONAL SABOTEUR. At once
Feodor wanted to die. He wondered how he could make
himself just die, efficiently and unobtrusively, so that
nobody in the already packed stands – their attention fixed
in anticipation on the dais by the river railings – would
notice the crumpling of an insignificant man in spectacles.
He was still wondering when a van drew up and a
handcuffed figure was let out of the back. The crowd set
up a great cheer which turned to laughter as people took in
the victim's bizarre appearance. The small figure was
dressed in a clown costume. The pantaloons came only to
mid-calf, exposing pale and defenceless shins to the
morning sun. The carnival atmosphere (for despite the
early hour ice-cream, hot dog and helium balloon vendors
were doing excellent business) was further complemented

by the oversized pair of coloured spectacles perched on the clown's red rubber nose. The plastic lenses were opaque with psychedelic spirals, a bloodshot eyeball painted in the centre of each. On his head was what any reader of *Mad* magazine in the Fifties could have identified as a propeller beanie.

In this awful figure Feodor had at once discerned his college friend. Until the van drew up it might all have been a joke or else the victim would turn out to be someone of the same name. But there was no mistaking the way Nicolai held himself, even in handcuffs with his eyes invisible behind the grotesque lenses and facing a hooting mob. This was recognisably the dandyish, even mocking, stance of the same beautiful young man who had once called him 'little Einstein of the tundra' with more affection than condescension. Failing the release of instant death Feodor now willed himself to faint. Whatever had to happen, he couldn't bear to watch. But his body willed otherwise and his eyes – which seemed quite impervious to whatever hideous image they might have to take in – followed Nicolai as he was led up on to the dais. For the first time Feodor allowed himself to see the thick iron bollard which jutted up behind. It was, in fact, merely one of hundreds of Napoleonic cannon which had been embedded vertically in the embankment and painted an ornamental green. To this the clown was strapped, facing the crowd. His escorts retreated. Now a squad of six militiamen with rifles filed smartly up in front and was halted by an officer.

At least, thought Feodor numbly, this ghastly charade would soon be over. Evidently the crowd thought so too and subsided with groans of disappointment. Hush fell. The sun was spanking quick gold tatters off the river surface. The distant roofs shone. The propeller on the clown's skullcap twirled in the breeze. Somewhere a dog barked. The officer held a sword aloft in his white-gloved hand and after a prodigious pause the blade fell. Six shots as one, six puffs of drifting smoke. The prisoner staggered but was supported by his straps. An incredulous laugh rang out, followed by others, until the whole crowd was roaring and pointing. Feodor's faithless eyes followed their fingers and saw long tongues of fine steel sticking out of five rifle muzzles. Swaying on the end of each was a flag reading 'Bang!'

Oh, this was popular stuff. On the clown's upper arm was a spreading crimson stain. The officer marched forward and inspected the victim before shaking his head in mock astonishment. The man who had fired the live round pretended shame at his poor marksmanship. The officer re-formed his firing squad, had them shoulder arms and marched them off with the flags nodding *Bang! Bang!* above their heads. Next, a van drove up with a red cross painted on its side and two nurses hopped out. They approached the wounded clown holding between them a huge piece of sticking plaster which they wrapped entirely around his upper body. More laughter. They and the ambulance retired, being replaced almost at once by a jeep from which equipment was unloaded. A man carried a metal box with a plunger which he set down in front of the crowd. He attached wires to two terminals and retreated to the dais, unspooling cable as he went. He fiddled with the wires behind the clown's back, presumably securing them to the cannon. Meanwhile, others were placing heavy screens around the dais. These had sinister mesh grilles in their upper halves so the victim's head was still visible to the crowd. The jeep backed off. The man walked to the black box and knelt before it, his back to the people. Suddenly his shoulders tensed, his hands drove the plunger home. The clown's head disappeared in a ball of smoke. 'Oh Nicky, oh thank God,' Feodor heard himself think exactly as three dyed pigeons burst upwards out of the smoke and circled the scene. One was blue, one was brown and the third was green. They were the colours of the national flag and represented the country's famous lakes, fertile soil and boundless forests. The crowd, scenting fresh trickery and postponement, were delighted. The clearing smoke soon revealed Nicolai's head, bowed but still intact, behind the grilles. Death by indignity? But what had been designed to prove fatal? The suspense was delicious.

A heavy, yellow-painted vehicle arrived, less a truck than a mobile base for some sort of maintenance platform on a telescopic pole. A soldier was already on the platform, which was simply a box enclosed by safety rails. It swung towards the dais. The clown was unshackled from the cannon and re-handcuffed. His face was black with explosive and a seepage of red had soaked through the moronic bandage. A noose was placed around his neck and spare coils of the rope heaped on to the platform while the free end was tied to the safety rails. Then he was helped into the cage with the soldier. Feodor thought there was also blood on the clown's earlobes; the explosion had probably ruptured the musician's eardrums. The truck's engine roared and the platform soared hydraulically into the sky on the end of its tapering pole of glistening steel. At maximum extension it stopped, swaying slightly against the blue sky in which the dyed pigeons still flew their brainless circles. The soldier could be seen urging the clown to climb out and then giving him an abrupt shove. Nicolai fell, trailing a black snake of rope. The propeller beanie came off and tumbled away on a pathetic trajectory of its own. But what was this? The rope was still lengthening even as the victim's plunge visibly slowed, hesitated, reversed itself. Upward sped the clown, newly fouled pantaloons fluttering with the rush of air, the bungee rope around his neck shrinking until his head almost struck the base of the platform from which he had just been pushed.

Later, Feodor learned that his friend had survived the mock hanging with a torn throat and neck injuries but that he'd still managed to keep on his feet to face two further attempts on his life. Feodor's own body had at last yielded to his mind and he had dropped unconscious in the stand.

'The heat. The crowd. The excitement. Don't worry, Dr Sarin. People were fainting everywhere. The authorities were overwhelmed by the popularity of the People's Disgrace, that's all. Next time they'll build bigger stands to accommodate more people in greater comfort. All the same, it's really a shame you missed the end.'

Feodor had tried hard not to learn the bestial means by which his friend had finally been despatched. Words such as 'sizzle' which slipped through his defences were at once thrown into a deep oubliette in his mind from which no images returned and in which no information was put together. The propeller beanie and clown's garb belonged to a nightmare pageant he'd heard about. Sweet Nicolai himself went on being his college friend, intact, laughing and drawing music in the gravel. Only when he thought of him at night Feodor heard a pure, far chord of D flat, the aching sound of limitless distances and separation.

But the search for the new National Anthem was still unfinished. The Academicians were not sold on any of the other tunes which had been entered and at last, despairing of finding one which combined musical catchiness and ideological purity, they hit on an interesting idea. Perhaps they had read a true account somewhere – or was it apocryphal, a pastiche Borges parable? – of how a harassed newspaper editor in some Latin or Central American country, despairing of trying to publish a daily news-sheet with the military junta's censors sitting in the office, did the logical thing, sent all his staff home and told the censors to write the paper themselves from headline to crossword. And now the Academicians did much the same. Feodor was summoned and told to write the tune himself. Quick as you can, they urged. No more messing about. It's got to be ready for the Martyrs' Day parades.

Who guards the guards? as the Roman sagely asked, and the National Anthem Co-ordinating Committee might have wondered the same thing had they had their wits about them. Even so, it was doubtful if anyone could have broken the exquisite cipher which Feodor now embedded, with infinite artistry, in his tune. Oh, it was adroitly done. One of the simplest tricks for deceiving the ear – if not also the eye – is to play a familiar tune with the correct notes but at the wrong octave. A smooth line becomes transformed into a jagged, aleatory-sounding jumble. Feodor now used just such a device, combining it with refined trickery besides distributing his passage between the voices so that it vanished. For all that he was no composer, he came up with a tune practically as good as poor Nicolai's. More stately, perhaps, but more easily learned by massed choirs. He set it in the unusual key of D flat but it was nearly always played in the brighter D.

Feodor received a medal for his tune, which proved hugely popular and soon came to stand for the nation at ceremonies the world over. The years went by until he realised at last that he was in the clear. Nobody now would dare examine his tune for political incorrectness. Even if some other bespectacled train-spotter with a strange mathematical bent for ciphers uncovered a suspicious sequence of notes and broke the code he would keep it to himself in the knowledge that if he didn't, a mere firing squad was too much to hope for. This mythical schoolboy would have discovered that the number 75009981 could be made to generate a substitution series, letters for notes, using the keywords 'Azovskiy Express'. After that it would only be a matter of time before he found, in the closing and triumphant phrase of the National Anthem, the equally mettlesome subtext 'People's Disgrace'.

Baḥḥ

WHEN IBRAHIM SALEH first saw the little apartment block
outlined against the mauve dusk rapidly deepening above
Tripoli he was relieved. In his experience his fellow
teachers tended to live in warren-like flats in the Old City:
hot, crowded apartments where children seeped like
cockroaches through holes in sprung doorframes and
walls. This building on the outskirts seemed at first sight a
more secure place. Indeed, from the crossroads on, the
road had reminded him of his own home near Abu Qir
outside Alexandria: a strip of threadbare asphalt bordered
by low white houses with stalls set up in front. Pressure
lamps flared above sticky piles of dates, gleamed off
vegetables and cooking pots. Here the palm trees easily
outnumbered the telegraph poles which some colonial
regime or other had planted the better to administer and
oppress the people whose land they had shamelessly
annexed; in this case presumably the Italians or the British.
On the far side of the crossroads was the suburb of luxury
villas where, in streets with names like *via* Verdone or *sciara*
Mazzini, the foreigners lived. On this side, though, lay the

southeastern area of town which was still more rural than urban, more *sha'bi* than bourgeois. Keep going along this road, Ibrahim knew, and one reached an extended oasis interspersed with orange groves, vineyards and olive plantations. This fertile but arid belt stretched out behind Tajura, inland from the Americans' vast air force base, Wheelus Field, and on for miles.

The headlamps of the modest Fiat he had borrowed – for who on a teacher's salary could afford to run a car? – flashed over crumbling drystone walls topped with prickly pear. Having left the asphalt he found himself on sand. Inexpertly he spun the wheels and sent the little car lurching around the building, narrowly missing a date palm with a tethered goat dozing at its foot. The creature's eyes winked bright yellow as he surged by. Ibrahim had some vague idea that by driving past the apartment block he would mislead any spies or police informers, then realised too late there was nowhere else to go. Worse, he caught the glow of oil lamps in hovels among the palms. It was hardly likely that his presence would have gone unnoticed. Irritated at having been forced by caution to draw attention to himself he kept the car going and drove entirely around the building, noting that at the back a sheer ten-foot wall surrounded the ground floor flat's garden. He came out at the front again and reluctantly parked.

Muntasser himself opened the door and reached for the crate of Mirinda orangeade which Ibrahim was cradling.

He led the way up three flights of stairs to the roof, the Egyptian following with the precious radio. The others were already there, sitting on mats with a tin tray of empty glasses. After the greetings Ibrahim asked '*Fi talj?*'

'I've sent Yunus for some,' Muntasser said. 'The butcher down the road sells it as a sideline. It's better value than his meat. When does the Colonel speak?'

'Seven o'clock,' said Ibrahim, slanting the tanned face of his ancient watch to catch the day's last (or the stars' earliest) light and failing. He knelt beneath the parapet and clicked his lighter. 'Ten minutes to go.' Within moments his son arrived, an eight-year-old carrying a heavy newspaper-wrapped package containing a block of ice rolled in yellow chaff. By the time several bottles of orangeade had been decanted into a brass ewer and mixed with lumps of ice Ibrahim had found Cairo on his radio and the martial music which heralded one of the President's thrilling speeches.

The group of teachers had recently taken to meeting each week in a succession of houses in order to listen to the Colonel as, indeed, his fervent admirers and hopeful nationalists listened all over the Arab world. 'He alone is a man,' as Ibrahim had said simply – had kept on saying, actually, to Muntasser's faint irritation which he dared not express. Ibrahim was, after all, the only Egyptian among them. Was there maybe the slightest suggestion that he mystically partook of his heroic compatriot's manhood whereas the rest of them (four Libyans and an Algerian

French teacher) didn't? This was, after all, 1966. While it was true that a whole decade had elapsed since Colonel Nasser had made total fools of the British, the French and the Israelis and had liberated both his country and the Suez Canal from their tyrannical grasp, it was also true that Algeria had thrown off the French yoke four years ago after a protracted and far crueller struggle. Ben Bella and the others were surely just as much men as Gamal Abdel Nasser; though one had to admit that if the Arab world had a spokesman and a focal point it was definitely Nasser and Cairo rather than Boumédienne and Algiers.

Up there on the roof much of the city's ambient glow was cut off by the low parapet. The men sat and sipped orangeade while listening to the tinny, hectoring voice, their eyes fixed unseeingly on a star, the spout of the ewer, the radio's grille. Now and again they would chorus assent or individually breathe a soft '*Y'Allah!*' Everything Nasser said about Israel, America and the international oil companies' client regimes struck the Libyans especially as having particular relevance. From the direction of Wheelus AFB down the coast came the intermittent faint thunder of Phantom F4s taking off for night bombing practice on the desert ranges, their pilots destined for an escalating war half the world away in a country called Vietnam. Every Libyan knew that King Idris – their own first-ever monarch – had been elevated with British backing from heading the Senussi clan to the throne of the newly independent state. Among students and the young

professionals who looked to Cairo for hope there was a
growing conviction that this puppet monarchy couldn't
last. Idris was old; it was known that he was ailing. He was
sometimes glimpsed in a limousine being whisked
towards Wheelus Field – for a weekly checkup at the Base
hospital, said the students. Some said he was already dead
and being impersonated by an actor while the British and
Americans worked out what to do; others that the figure
they saw, its right hand feebly raised in salute behind
tinted glass, was indeed that of the King, but *stuffed*. Oh,
these were heady times. Any day now, nobody doubted,
Colonel Nasser would lead a vast army of the massed Arab
nations to victory over Israel and liberate the Palestinian
people. Nobody listening to him up on the roof in Tripoli
doubted that they themselves, like millions of other
Maghribi volunteers, would be whisked magically to the
distant battlefield to shed their ounce of blood and partake
in the triumph.

In the middle of all this a large car chugged to a halt down
below and doors slammed. Muntasser stood quietly up and
peeped over the parapet. The others glanced at him but
lost interest again as with a shake of his head he returned to
his seat on the mat. Since he lived here he must have
recognised the car. One couldn't be too careful. These
days, with the regime getting jittery and student leaders
disappearing, it was safer to pretend the security police
were smarter than they actually were. Ten minutes went
by in which the slight interruption was forgotten. Other

than Nasser's unflagging voice (which had been known to go on for over three hours at a stretch, unrivalled except by Fidel Castro) there was little noise. So the intrusive sound, when it started, jarred the listeners' state of being both uplifted and lulled by oratory. The men came out of their trance and looked at Muntasser.

'That's the foreigner on the ground floor,' he said apologetically.

'Great God. Does he do this every night?'

'Most nights, yes. It's a piano. He hired it from Frugoni's.'

They tried to retrieve their concentration but the Colonel's exhortations had done their work. The sheer immediacy of this alien intrusion was all the more piquing for its extraordinary punctuality. What was this if not the cultural outreach of neocolonialism? The music meandered loudly on, full of disagreeable harmonic clashes. It rose pungently from below like the odour of foreign cooking, its obtrusiveness amplified the building's design. The instrument was evidently in the back room and being played with the doors wide open. The sound was collected by the garden's high cement walls and thrown upwards.

'Who is this person? Have you complained?'

'Not really,' Muntasser admitted, but immediately realised this sounded feeble. 'I mean, I've told him how audible it is. I was hoping he might take the hint. He's a Briton. He works for the British Council.'

'Does he just.' Ibrahim was stern. He looked over the parapet, both palms firmly planted. 'Is he married?'

'No.'

'Well, he has two girls down there in the garden walking around in shameless dresses. Two.'

'Yunus sells him eggs,' Muntasser offered. 'We keep hens. I cleared them out for our meeting here tonight but normally they live up here. Yunus says the man's taught him to write "Yunus" on a typewriter.'

'Has he. Next thing you know he'll be teaching the boy the Bible. Or the piano, which would be almost as bad. What a racket! Imagine listening to this for pleasure when you could be listening to Umm Kulsum! I don't mind these foreigners being corrupt or infidel,' said Ibrahim with a show of Egyptian good-humoured sophistication which he knew would slightly annoy his companions, 'that's their business. But they're so different you can't really get to grips with them. They might as well be from Mars. Look at Jackson.'

Jackson was one of the four British teachers in their government school, paid to teach English by direct method. Jackson was tall, bald, cavernous and from Newcastle. Nobody, not even his fellow countrymen, understood a word he said. There was a rumour that he'd induced two of his students to perform unnatural acts with him in return for a good examination result; but one had failed while the other passed and besides, nobody could quite believe it of him. Jackson seemed about as erotically motivated as a date palm, which had to be mated by hand. An enigma, in short.

'The others aren't so bad.'

'Well no, they're not,' Ibrahim agreed. 'So far as you can make them out, they're nice enough as individuals.' A fresh jangle of notes rushed upwards. 'But the Colonel's right. It's what they *stand* for which threatens us all. What's the British Council if not a propaganda wing of the British Government? That piano's its Trojan Horse, if you ask me.'

This made everyone laugh a little uneasily.

'He says it's *Baḥḥ*,' Muntasser volunteered after a pause.

'What's that supposed to mean?'

'I don't know. He said "There's nothing like a bit of *Baḥḥ* in the evenings." '

'I'm glad to hear it. The thought that there might be anything else like this is chilling indeed.' More laughter. 'Those women. I suppose they're Sicilian hussies?'

By now the others had joined him at the parapet. They looked down into the enclosed area three floors below. The inside of the garden walls had been rendered and painted cream. Although nobody was actually standing outside on the arid patch of soil two indistinct shadows were cast against the end wall by the lights from the downstairs room. The shadows came together, maybe a hand reached out – one of the blurs grew a sudden limb like an elephant's trunk up by its head – the bodies merged. The conspirators up there among the stars watched the wall as if it were a cinema screen, the relentless drone of notes the accompanying soundtrack to a foreign film which at any moment might become terrifyingly licentious. They couldn't tear their eyes away. Behind them on the low table Colonel Nasser earnestly harangued a bottle opener and a heap of wet newsprint covered in chaff.

'Was one of the girls blonde?' enquired Muntasser at length.

'Both,' said Ibrahim tersely.

'Then I know who they are. Nurses. They've been here before.'

'For a spot of *Baḥḥ*? One day I'm going to receive a telegram informing me that my father wasn't actually a melon grower at all but a Saudi prince. The mistake has been acknowledged and can only be rectified by my leading a life of total erotic indulgence. In fact, non-stop *Baḥḥ*. Only thus will I be able to forget foreigners half my age who have girls and cars and four times my salary.'

It was not easy to judge Ibrahim, his colleagues were thinking. In his way he, too, was a foreigner. He had this black Egyptian humour. One was never quite sure where laughter turned into anger, if indeed it did. It might just be that mock anger was part of his humorous mode. There were other areas of uncertainty, too. He made no secret of his socialist leanings and seemed to know outright Marxists back home. But Marx had very pronounced views on religion; and whereas a man's private relationship with God was nobody else's business, the suspicion about Ibrahim was that he was probably rather secular. He had a habit of saying shocking things, as when he mentioned the cars parked at night off the coast road, their noses pointing seawards, their windows wound up except now and then when a crack would open to let an empty beer or whisky bottle thump on to the sand. The Libyans were conservative; there were things one didn't mention. They didn't need an Egyptian to point out that these were not foreigners indulging in secret drinking, parked at safe twenty-yard intervals so no-one could recognise anybody else. It wasn't foreigners who dared not drink at home, any more than it was foreigners who sent away their maids before midday during Ramadan so nobody would see them when they came back from the office at two to raid the fridge. It was Ibrahim who now and then made bitter references to hypocrisy, only retrieving things by adding that it was all part of the corrupting influence of the West which would be swept away when Nasserism embraced and liberated the Arab peoples.

The noise down below had stopped. Once more they peered over the edge and were just in time to see the man emerge with the two girls. Each carried a glass. Voices began to float up with awesome clarity so that even the Algerian teacher could more or less follow their English.

'I love your lawn.'

'Thanks; I have this terrible problem with clover. But you must admit the rhodies are looking fairly splendid this year.'

'*And* your peonies . . .'

'Masses and masses of blooms.'

There was laughter as the three wandered the bald square of compacted earth.

'These nights!' one of the girls said. 'They're so sultry. Lovely smell. Sort of scented.'

'It's the orange trees on the remaining Italian estates which haven't gone back to desert. You can smell them for miles at night.'

'Not a bit like Letchworth, is it, Chrissie? It makes me want to *do* something. That's the trouble with Trippers. There's buggerall to do here in the evenings.'

'Except *Baḥḥ*,' fiercely murmured Ibrahim overhead.

'You know I was in Cairo last year?'

'Wasn't that dangerous, Tim? We Brits are hardly popular with the good Colonel, I should think.'

'Oh, I wasn't there as a Council officer, obviously. Just as a private citizen, a visitor. In any case the Egyptians're the sweetest people.'

'*Nasser's* a sweet person?' asked one of the girls.

'He's the biggest pussy-cat of them all. He just gets a bit carried away if he's given a microphone. I spent an evening with a close friend of his, a newspaper editor called Mohamed Heikal. We went to this splendid run-down hotel full of potted palms and old servants in *galabeyas* which had a nightclub. At least, that's what it was called. It was quite the most wonderful place I've ever been in. Terrifically gloomy, just a scattering of little tables each with a candle, and some stout middle-aged women with split skirts. But the *pièce de résistance* was the band, a sort of *thé dansant* quintet which couldn't have changed since the Thirties. I'm not kidding – they wore red fezzes and played tangos while some piggy Russians shuffled about on the floor with the ladies in split skirts. I fell in love with that hotel. The man behind the reception desk had once shaken hands with Winston Churchill and there was a dusty photograph on the wall to prove it. In his youth he'd been Egypt's fastest Pyramid-runner. They used to do it for the tourists – run up and down the Great Pyramid. Not an easy way to earn a living if you think about it. Not just the awful height, plus the steepness and the heat, but there's so much casing missing. You have to scramble up huge blocks of stone here and there. Anyway, this fellow nipped up and down for Churchill in a record time that was never beaten. Probably never will be, now, since you're no longer allowed to do it. Anyway, when I first came to Tripoli I looked high and low for an equivalent of that hotel but I'm afraid it doesn't exist.'

'There's a nightclub in the Waddan, someone said.'

'It's not in the same league. They play "Stupid Cupid" and "Che sarà, sarà" and it's full of Yugoslav whores and oil men with crew-cuts and beer bellies. Completely uncivilised. The essential thing is that mournful atmosphere of decayed gentility, of being in a time-warp. The Waddan's nothing but oil-money-meets-frontier-town. It's brash and expensive and completely without echoes of any kind. No, I should like to spend the rest of my life in Cairo. I could never go back to England now, but I think I could easily live in Groppi's.'

Of the eavesdroppers on the roof, most had got the gist; Ibrahim had understood everything. His head trembled in the starlight. What was he to think? It was disarming to hear his country described in such affectionate terms. At the same time, to hear Colonel Nasser called a pussy-cat was insulting and condescending beyond measure. Yet if he were to be believed, this cocky young Briton had apparently sat in a nightclub with Heikal himself, one of the Revolution's most illustrious intellectuals . . . Nothing added up. Probably it was all lies. On the other hand . . .

'Just thank your lucky stars we're not in Riyadh,' Tim was saying down below. 'At least here we can all have another glass of wine and take our clothes off if we feel like it.'

'Not a bad idea.'

'Still, it would be better done indoors. Discretion and all that. It's one of those countries where you have to fall back on your own resources. Unless you're inventive you find yourself spending hours just wandering around Mitchell Cotts' supermarket picking conversations about Ovaltine and Marmite with oil wives. Or waiting for Scottish Country Dancing night to come round at the Elizabethan. It's not on. So – more wine. And more *Baḥḥ*. No, better still, let's try some Noël Coward.'

The three foreigners trooped back inside. Soon came the sound of muffled laughter and once again ambiguous shadows lunged and melded on the garden wall. Some random notes were played on the piano and then came singing: the man, the two girls, loud giggles. This sort of music didn't strike the watchers as quite so alien. You could hear noises like these when you tuned in the wrong station on the radio. That earlier stuff without the human voice was like nothing on earth. Reluctantly they turned back to the remains of the Mirinda, now flat and warm. A curious depression had swept up over them, as if the easterly zephyrs which had earlier brought the scent of citrus groves had backed and was now the carrier of a mephitic listlessness. Ibrahim turned off Cairo Radio to save the batteries. Nobody objected.

'If they're singing they can't be having sex.'

'Probably not.' This was slightly consoling.

Low on the eastern horizon a bright light appeared, flaring and trembling like a diamond on a jeweller's cushion. An American Air Force transport banking into its final approach.

'I'll ask him tomorrow,' said Muntasser at length. ' "Please close your windows, Mr Tim, when you play your piano at night. There are young children in the house trying to sleep." He speaks quite good Arabic. He's always very reasonable.'

'Pah,' said Ibrahim. He gathered up his radio. 'We shan't meet here again. It's too unsafe. It's not your fault,

Muntasser. A man must live somewhere. Who was to know a foreigner would choose to live here instead of in Garden City?'

Muntasser let him out again, carrying the crate of empties with the radio on top. The bare hallway echoed to the singing behind the door of the ground floor flat. Outside the building Ibrahim found a vast American car whose rump sprouted fishing-rod aerials. The Egyptian climbed mournfully into the borrowed Fiat, belching orange-flavoured carbon dioxide which made his eyes water. He started the car and drove off. Not unsafe, he corrected himself mentally. The building was less unsafe than contaminated. He wished the man Tim hadn't spoken so fondly of Egypt. He would pass on a word or two about him. If he'd really sat around in Cairo hotels with Heikal he was working for somebody. He would need watching.

And that went equally for this *Baḥḥ* . . . Whatever it might be – sexual practice, social convention, cultural tradition – it represented an area of unease. He must discover as soon as possible what it was without revealing a degree of ignorance that might provoke scorn. As he drove slowly down towards the seafront Ibrahim found all his own uncertainty and cross-purposes, his hardness towards nations and his softness towards people, had coalesced around this mysterious *Baḥḥ* until it took on the threat of ruination. He suddenly realised he wanted a woman, right now, something swift and clear and absorbing to drive away the evening's unease. There ought to be some Syrian whores in the *maidan*. It was no fun being in exile, seconded by one's government to teach for a pittance in what was frankly a benighted backwater, far away from wife and family. Another two whole years . . . He wished the Englishman hadn't mentioned Groppi's. The famous Cairo café painfully reminded Ibrahim of his favourite Alexandria watering-holes: Pastroudis and the Hotel Cecil; the Crazy Horse nightclub on Ramleh Square with Dr Alky and his band, The Frogs, accompanying oriental dances . . .

Well, he thought as he turned westward along the seafront to the older part of town, it would soon be time for action. Some of his own students were raring to go. It was a matter of selecting targets. Oil company offices, lone American servicemen, those fatherless Italian slavers on their estates. What was that place Tim had said the British went to at night? The Elizabethan Club. When that went up in flames, Ibrahim reflected, it ought to take a tidy bit of *Baḥḥ* with it . . . But just then his attention was diverted by the strollers along the sea-wall. Failing a Syrian whore there was always one of those rich foreign men in tight white trousers simply begging for it.

Sidonie Kleist

SINCE I'M a prisoner of Chinese nuns, let us examine the *double entendres* of the words 'cell', 'asylum', and 'sanctuary' . . . No, on second thoughts let's just describe the calendar on the wall. It would gladden the heart of any musician, being inscribed with the name 'C-sharp Spectacle Co.'. The days and months are in both Chinese and Roman: good-luck red in the case of the Chinese and mournful blue for the Roman lettering, which maybe has something to say about Eastern optimism and Western pessimism, hope and nostalgia, looking forwards and looking back. In any case the bilingual, bi-cultural efficiency is further enhanced by the industriousness suggested in a running legend 'Sun Wah Tsui Optical Laboratories' and a Hong Kong address. Why, then, did these nifty entrepreneurs – whom I visualise seeing sharply ahead through a pair of their own spectacles – provide their calendar with a picture so fatally tainted with backwardness?

It is a colour photograph, about a foot square, of a model Nativity scene (plaster? plastic?) of which only the foreground is in focus. Clumps of ferns, unquestionably plastic and of that virulent green of children's drinks, surround a sort of coral outcrop. Against this is posed a shiny pink *putto* with a heavily made-up face, rouged nipples too high up its chest and wearing a pair of golden knickers which mercifully hide what would otherwise be chubby and winsome genitalia. From this horrid infant's curls grows a fringe of gilded antlers, presumably beams of glory, and on one upraised palm sits a white pigeon. Boy and bird are gazing at each other with sickly intimacy. Try as we might, we can't convince ourselves that the kid is going to wring the animal's neck and give it to his soft-focus mother in the background to cook for lunch. Nor do we imagine the bird is going to have the wit to shit on this frightful effigy as its living counterparts do on statues the world over to show nature's contempt for human hubris.

How vile the Holy Family was, is, and always will be. Imagine: this rancid scene claims to depict the home life of the Lord of the Universe, guaranteeing that anyone with the slightest taste takes her devotional custom elsewhere. I know little enough about Islam but I do know it has the decorum to outlaw representations of God. I also know, from the days when it was still possible for an American woman to wander in Iran, how breathtakingly beautiful were the abstract designs in many mosques: intellectual and aesthetic riches which constantly drew the mind outwards. By contrast this iconography of the basic domestic unit is the debased fag-end of Renaissance shlock, a sort of idealised quattrocento Italian *famiglia*: kiddie-widdie, daddy-waddy, wifey-poo. All that's lacking is a doggy-woggy, though there are baa-lambs and, of course, the representation of the Holy Spirit as potential Sunday roast. I'm fed up from ass to tonsils with Renaissance art. All of it.

So what happens when you're a professional concert pianist and you wake up one day to discover you're irrevocably out of love with your own culture? Oh, never mind the cuisine and the sexual customs; I mean the arts, the whole grand European edifice which supposedly speaks for the world's zillions. What happened in my case was that I froze in the middle of Beethoven's Fourth piano concerto and had to be carried offstage like Euridice to Hades while Orpheus – temporarily disguised as Chou Mei Ling, the conductor – gazed after me with helpless consternation. That I do remember. Less clear is the series of darkened rooms through which I passed *en route* to this airy retreat and/or prison high above Kwun Tong. 'Gastric collapse', the *South China Morning Post* called it, having been told to, since nervous breakdowns are as impermissible onstage as technical ones. 'A spiritual crisis', cheerfully says Sister Lotus Blossom who brings me pots of green tea. She's not really called that, I'm just mocking my upbringing. She's sweet and has those spectacles (quite possibly in C sharp) which nuns always seem to wear: nearly rimless except for bits of gold wire. My fingers itch to lift them off her nose like a Cary Grant businessman in a Hollywood movie ('Why, Sister, has anybody ever told you how beautiful you are?') and replace them with silver-coated microcorneal lenses, sexy and sinister. In my next incarnation I'm definitely not going to be lesbian. It was a category thrust upon me by the times in which I lived, as were 'American' and 'concert pianist'. Next time I shall be a free agent in a frontierless world. My disgust with the familial will make a good start.

Why should a brief account of my personal *crise* be of the least interest? Yet Mother Ignatia insists on it since I can't at the moment talk. Or won't; I myself don't know which. Evidently my sudden refusal to make public sounds goes further than merely abandoning my career in a minor key, unable even to begin the Finale. Ignatia's a very sensible person and wants at all costs to keep me out of the hands of psychiatrists. 'What do they understand about art?' she asks. 'They think despair is just a matter of chemical imbalance. Are we to dissolve our grief and remorse with little pills? Perhaps Beethoven would never have written his music if he'd been fed little pills.' This is quite likely but so what? If little pills can stop people being unhappy then I'm all for them even if it means fewer concertos. In any case Mother Iggy knows the details of my 'collapse' and attaches great importance to them. 'Why that piece?' she keeps asking. 'Why *there*, just before the last movement? Go on, write it down. You've all the time in the world.'

And so I look back, and reflect on the consequences of looking back, even as I move about my pleasant white dungeon gazing now at the fearful calendar and now out of the window at the restless construction site which is the latest New World. Even for Mother Iggy I can't summon the energy to put down yet again a version of the autobiography which satisfies those journalists who do their profiles of concert hall artists. They accord much significance to the prodigy in plaits, the school prizes, the Juilliard moppet, the Big Break. I don't say this person never existed or the facts are incorrect; she did but she wasn't me, they aren't incorrect but neither are they truthful. Sidonie Kleist the pianist is not Sidonie Kleist the speechless captive of the Order of Intercessionists in Hong Kong.

My Doubts (and even I can't avoid the religious overtones of a faltering faith) began in earnest with the aforesaid Big Break. This was a recording of Beethoven's Fourth piano concerto – what else? – for whose ludicrous success I can't offer a unitary explanation. Okay, it was an interesting if mannered reading of the work but it was *packaged*: that's the only phrase for it. For a start, the posters showed a larger version of the picture on the CD which pretty much broke with tradition. In it I'm not gazing meditatively into a grand piano, or conferring between takes with a shirtsleeved conductor. It was actually a holiday photo taken on a visit to Arran. I'm sitting on a creel in a pretty granite harbour, gutting fish. I'm caught in the act, bloody fingers inside a mackerel, wicked knife in one hand, a drool of intestines hanging towards my lap. I happened that day (which was unseasonably hot) to be wearing a Juilliard T-shirt, the only overt link with music in the picture. I don't know why the photo was so effective, though I've been told it tapped into a certain feminist current, the notion of specifically female readings of the classical repertoire, since it purported to show a capable individual neither squeamish nor frightened of cutting her delicate, highly insured digits. A change from the usual fragile warriors of the keyboard? Who knows?

What I do know about my performance, retrospectively, is that it was even more artful than the choice of the picture. I should like the bandwagon-load of critics who praised it so extravagantly to know that it was as molecularly engineered as any new pharmaceutical. What is incredible to me now is that in some peculiar fashion I managed to conceal this from myself. I really believed I was turning in an original performance, a vision of Beethoven uniquely mine. Bullshit. I already had an established career, of course; the fact that I was under contract to a record company meant I'd jumped that first hurdle and no longer needed to worry about doing sessions work for a living. The big league was the next stage and I was being groomed for it. Whether pre- or post-grooming, anyway, it's a romantic fiction to pretend one's account of any piece of music with almost two centuries of performance behind it can ever be uniquely one's own.

I don't know how much of a music buff Mother Ignatia

is, so can't guess whether she'll be shocked to discover how cynically that recording of mine was prepared. For a start we have to dodge uneasily around the question which becomes more insistent year by year: *Who needs another recording of Beethoven 4?* Or his symphonies, violin concerto or whatever? Or hundreds of other works, come to that, from Pachelbel's canon (I think its popularity was just a fad) to Brahms 1 and 4? So what new *could* anybody say about the Beethoven G major? Because this is the point, obviously. With God knows how many recordings of B4 being released each year to compete for attention you've got to have an angle, what the ad industry calls a Unique Selling Point. I happened to have been reading Owen Jander and was talking about the concerto in terms of programme music. The producer latched on to this pretty fast, scenting a USP. It's *programme* music? You mean like the Pastoral symphony? So I gave them this spiel about the contemporary fascination in Vienna with Ovid's *Metamorphoses* and the Orphic legend in particular, and how Beethoven himself became interested enough to write his concerto so that its three movements corresponded to the legend's three parts: the Song of Orpheus, Orpheus losing Euridice in Hades and Orpheus and the Bacchantes.

'Go for it!' he said. 'It's always called his most *lyrical* piano concerto. You can major in that.'

'Lyres?' I said. 'How would it be if I spread that first chord as an arpeggio instead of playing it cold? Like this . . .'

Agent, producer, conductor: they all loved it, especially after some scholarly argy-bargy about authenticity. This performance was going to be *different*, right from the first chord. As for the second movement, that was a knockout. No longer was it abstract music, a stark dialogue between orchestra and piano. This was human drama, really operatic in its recitative effects. Poor Orpheus tries his best to woo the Furies with his fragmented melancholy song, and actually wins Euridice her reprieve. He can bring her up from Hades provided he never looks back to see if she's following. But of course he does, just as Lot's wife did, because telling someone not to look back's like telling her on no account to think of elephants. Is it clear from the music when this fatal moment occurs? You bet it is, in my version. It's the anguished chromatic scales against a trill on C with the left hand crossing over to make two despairing cries in measures 56-59. After that the passionate lament grows still as the note-values double and redouble, to be followed not by the orchestral Furies howling in triumph as they undoubtedly would have in Berlioz but soft, as if they were stifled by remorse.

After this emotional climax there is, as always, the problem of the Finale. Not just a problem for us performers, either. It was a problem for composers from Haydn on: how to follow a really serious slow movement without destroying its effect. For example, people have bent over backwards to convince late-twentieth-century ears that there isn't a degree of *galant* triviality in the last movement of Mozart's G minor string quintet; that its emotionally neutral, tripping lyricism really is the perfect foil to the most despairing music he ever wrote, the most nihilistic in the whole Western canon. So what to do with the Beethoven Finale? My – or our – answer was to play it slightly hushed, to dim the glitter, restrain the romp. We scrupulously observed all Beethoven's sforzandos and orchestral outbursts, since violence was an integral part of his aesthetic; but they were relative rather than absolute. After all, nobody comes too well out of the original story. Euridice is lost for ever in Hades; the Bacchantes destroy Orpheus and are promptly punished by being turned into oak trees. The story may be muffled in tone but it's violent in import and that's the effect of my performance.

The critics ate it. Recording of the Year. Awards, acclaim. Ominous signs that Beethoven 4 might become known as 'Orpheus', much as Mozart 21 became temporarily known by the name of an otherwise forgettable movie. Engagements. More specifically, requests which – had I agreed to them – would have had me playing the concerto 528 times worldwide in two years. At that moment I began to take seriously the fate, or triumph, of Glenn Gould who from the time his first recording of it was released could have made a handsome living playing nothing but the *Goldberg Variations*. Gould's a figure with whom every pianist sooner or later has to come to terms since his career, whizzing wilfully along at a seeming tangent to everyone else's, still managed to whack head-on into major questions such as whether public performance is necessary or desirable, or if an ideal performance can be recorded by constructing it piecemeal from a mass of short takes. These issues are so radical and so germane that it suddenly seemed Gould might after all be the central figure among the last half-century's performers while everyone else was marginal in their avoidance of them.

An hour ago Sister Lotus Blossom took me to see Mother Iggy who smiled and asked if I might as a great favour play the harmonium for Compline. I truly hoped to smile as much as she, but try as I would I couldn't make either my mouth or my fingers move. Experimentally she laid my hands on the keys and switched the thing on with a little gassy roar for, incredible though it may seem, this Hong Kong order has no Yamaha keyboard, all lights and buttons, but a genuine pre-war Hammond with chunky stops labelled Vox Humana and Dulciana. When nothing happened she switched off.

'That was stupid of me,' she admitted. 'I don't know why I did that. If you'd been able to play would I pretend you were "cured" now, that everything was back to normal? I think it's a cliché taken from the cinema' (you can tell these Hong Kong nuns have been British-educated), 'this idea that when someone has an accident or a collapse they have to resume their old life as soon as possible. But maybe Sidonie Kleist *should* never play again. Maybe God has other plans for her.'

Oh, they're crafty, these religious. Until that final sentence I'd been thinking what an uncommonly sensible person she was. But with that little sally about God I tried everything I knew to voice the repartee which ached to come out. Alas, nothing came. I'm not even sure my mouth opened. Inwardly, I had my question perfectly formed: Had I been one of her Sisters who'd suddenly lost her faith would Mother Ignatia say, 'Oh, never mind, my dear. Maybe it's God's way of telling you to become an atheist'?

But to return to my own loss of cultural faith. As I said, it began with that momentous damned recording, actually right there in the studios. It was an unashamed bid for commercial success, an attempt to hijack Beethoven 4, to annexe it so that Sidonie Kleist's account would be required listening. There's a very principled British recording company which even now likes to record with a single microphone and in one take if at all possible. In other words it's committed to the inspiration of performance, fluffs and all, on the grounds that the idea of a definitive recording is absurd and one might as well aim for unity and spontaneity. Well, our approach to Beethoven 4 was the polar opposite, pretty much Gouldian. There were microphones everywhere. Groups of instruments were individually miked. The real performance took place afterwards, with balance engineers turning up this and fading down that, splicing in a note here and redubbing there until the final mix (sixty-four tracks, I think someone said). The result was nothing like what the conductor had heard or I'd played. What, come to that, did it have to do with Beethoven's concerto which until then I'd deeply loved since childhood? Forget integrity of performance, inspiration of the moment: all that was left of them was stray clumps of notes, odd quavers and minims drifting in the dead studio air like fur after a dog-fight. So all this prompted my question, which goes unanswered to this day: Where is the composer's voice? Or where the soloist's? (And have you ever wondered, as you whistle your bit of Mozart in the supermarket, whose performance it is? You're not a musician? So how did you know what tempo to adopt? Is it an average of all the recordings you've heard or is it your Soul up there on an inner podium?) In any case, the true voice behind my publicity shot of the fiercely individual artist gutting fish was neither Ludwig's nor Sidonie's but the record company's: a thin, opportunistic character utterly lacking in intellect but perfectly capturing the sound of the times. As soon as I realised this I was horrified. The paradox was perfect. This up-to-the-minute new account of Beethoven 4 was already dated, and me with it.

Instead of becoming angry with myself I became glum, and reading the critics enthusing over my playing in subsequent concerts and recitals made me glummer still. It seemed I could suddenly do no wrong even though my playing was unchanged. 'Sidonie Kleist's deft touches of dry humour' – what *could* it mean? A memory lapse in a Mozart concerto I was playing in London ought to have been pounced on as at least a lack of concentration. It was in the first movement recapitulation and I found myself inadvertently trying to drag us all back into the dominant again, locked into a cycle of repetition I couldn't break. I floundered for about five measures, hoping to make my F sharp sound like an interesting piece of chromatic intensification instead of the leading note of a now-unwanted G major. Did the critics notice? Did they hell. 'She just never puts a finger wrong' (*S. Times*). And even if she *did* never put a finger wrong, so what? What has playing the right notes to do with playing them correctly? 'Even her wrong notes sounded right' would satisfy me for an epitaph if someone would only say it in time.

It's all a farce.

One can't be a professional musician for long without becoming a cynic. There's the industry and there's the marketplace, and that's about it. People rely on critics to tell them which recordings to buy, what fashion, what image. How can they rely on their ears when even most critics couldn't tell Pavarotti from Carreras in a blindfold test, let alone Arrau from Barenboim? Cars, detergents, pharmaceuticals, artists.

It's hot. Outside the window there's a constant sullen roaring like an immense forest fire, a landscape ablaze. From where I'm sitting I see orange smoke drifting across a bald blue wash into which slender white rectangles thrust up their unequal tops. Framed in the window they look like a bar chart, statistics of an indefinite economy or an uncertain future. I get up and walk over and there are the new tower blocks jostling up and down the hillside. The smoke is dust from excavators gnawing away at rock, from trucks dumping sand and cement. The roar is of a city recycling itself and expanding, mixed with the vast exhalation of Kai Tak airport throwing up its haze of burnt kerosene and airplanes which drone at steep angles between the apartment blocks like leaden darts. I've little faith that it's all going somewhere. It seems to me as securely locked into frantic repetition as my own concertizing, our cultural treadmill. If I can't (or won't) speak or play then I must break with what no longer needs to be said and played. What does it mean to go on and on playing the same music over and over again? What does it really mean?

Hotel bedrooms.

And now a nunnery. They're called Intercessionists because they believe in a figure they describe as Our Lady of Perpetual Intercession. At any time of day or night, year in, year out, there are two nuns at prayer in the chapel. They do it in shifts. Mother Ignatia explains that it's a tenet of their faith: as long as there's someone somewhere on earth remaining in contact with God then the lines to redemption remain open and it can all go on. But if for a single instant that contact between God and humankind is broken (a backward, wistful glance towards Hades, a chance hiatus like one of those lulls in conversation at a dinner party), then we're lost and Satan's meat. That's why there are always two nuns, in case one of them has a heart attack or a stroke. So a constant thin smoke of prayer rises from the chapel downstairs and outside the airplanes can keep taking off and the buildings going up, concerts can be given and the world turns. They're very reassuring, these tribal magicians, these shamans who labour on everyone's behalf to keep the sky from falling, whose spells so successfully bid the sun rise and set. It's a kindly thought to use such prodigious power so beneficently.

The question is, will it one day strike Mother Iggy too, this awesome moment which silenced me? Why mightn't it suddenly overwhelm her, the sound in her own ears of the same words endlessly repeated until nothing but emptiness remains? I'd played at being Orpheus for two movements before looking back, and the world stopped. Music froze, a pillar of salt, a boulder of loss. There was no going on. I'd looked back and seen that everything I was belonged to the past. We'd all of us simultaneously – orchestra and audience – reached the end of our culture.

After my first week here, or maybe month, Mother Iggy asked me if I'd like to play something for the Sisters, a nice Mozart sonata perhaps? This was after the Hammond organ experiment so evidently hope springs eternal in her moviegoer's breast. I managed a small scream, the only sound I've uttered since the concert. How else was I to tell her how sick I am of our Mozart sonatas? 'Our' because of the way we've appropriated them; because what he wrote isn't what we play. Oh, the notes are probably the same but the eighteenth century heard something quite else. It was a different world with different ears. What once had the freshness of innovation has now hardened into a sacred fossil, an icon, a plaster *putto*, a consumer artefact which can never now transcend itself no matter how tricksily played.

That's true of all art, of course. Same for Shakespeare, same for Dante. What they really meant is forever lost to us. They've become medieval incantations heaved in a technological age. Time to break with this thumb-sucking, this churning round and round of the same great creaking prayer-wheel. That was then; this is now. No looking back. Devise a new language to talk. New things to say, even, instead of heaving our contemporary sighs into ancient deflated bladders until they take on a semblance of what we think is eternal. What needs to be said today isn't like anything which needed to be said before. We've never been on the lip of extinction until now. And who brought us to this calamitous point? Not just science or greed or the autoworkers of Detroit but the Holy Family, Michelangelo and Beethoven too. They're all part of it. But don't worry: new geniuses will invent new fantasies for us to believe in, other truths to bring us to our knees or fill our eyes with astonished tears. So have confidence, good Mother. Satan will no more take over your phone network than a new barbarism will rush in to fill the space left by Beethoven.

It is I, Orpheus, who speaks. It is I, Sidonie Kleist, who can tell you that after a certain amount of fun with the Bacchantes and the strong drink etc., which brings oblivion, Orpheus gave up the lyre and became a pirate. This is not well known. He lived rough and saw much. He took what he fancied and left what he didn't and had a fine, long, unencumbered life. Now and then he wondered how Euridice was doing down there in Hades and reflected that she'd been quite a canny, headstrong girl and probably had life with the Furies pretty much psyched out. The former lyrist had been a reflective sort of fellow, which was one of the reasons for choosing a piratical career since his new colleagues were refreshingly disinclined to the backward glance. But eventually Orph the morph worked out what had really been pretty damned obvious all along: that he'd looked back on the road out of Hades quite deliberately *in order to be rid* of Euridice. We're constantly changing and *eheu!* he'd outgrown her. He'd played a lot of lyre and he'd outgrown that, too. All legends have domestic origins which become lost. So he kept absolutely silent about the whole thing, never joined in with the shanties in the fo'c'sle and otherwise successfully transcended his former self.

There's a lesson here for us all.

Farts and Longing

'IT's *YOU*, isn't it?'

I'm probably destined to blurt this whenever I meet him, in a mixture of sheer surprise, pleasure and pride. Pride, because I'm the only person he'll talk to – or so he claims. This amounts to a privilege so singular that in a way I'm a genius myself on the strength of it, if a passive one. On the other hand I now have a far better idea of the hollowness and relativity of the very notion of 'genius', so I hardly ever use the term now except mockingly. Come to that, mockery is something I'm well acquainted with, obviously. But how could I have kept silent? When I described my first conversation with him I was treated with the indulgence due the disturbed: yet one of the details I recounted did finally percolate through to the world of scholarship and occasion a good solid discovery. Naturally the scholar concerned attributed it to his own insight rather than to my article which I know he'd read. Never mind, I thought. There'll be another time.

To know this is still no preparation for when it happens. On this latest occasion it was evening and I was nursing a beer and watching Malta's desert-hued rocks turn rosy. A huge flattened sun was cautiously lowering itself into the sea like a courtesan easing her buttocks into an over-hot bath. The holiday crowds had mostly shuffled off the beach to shake the sand from their towels on to hotel carpets and anoint each other's smarting shoulders in preparation for the disco. A tall black man approached my solitary table. He was gorgeously dressed in tribal robes whose provenance I couldn't guess. In my mind I confused him vaguely with all the Libyans who came shuttling through Valletta from Tripoli, often wealthy families heading for Harrods or the London Clinic and reduced by a capricious embargo to undertake the first leg of their journey on a ferry. He bent so that his pale blue headdress came below the edge of the Martini umbrella. I noticed he was holding a thin journal of sorts rolled up in one hand.

'I'm Tom Abandanaya,' he said. 'From Lagos, actually. Would you mind if I joined you?'

'Er . . . no, of course,' I said with the fretful courtesy of an Englishman taken by surprise. 'Sit down, by all means. Can I offer you a beer? Or maybe you're . . .'

'A Muslim? No, I'm a lapsed everything. A beer would be fine.'

The waiter poured it, grinning into the sunset as the rosy foam climbed the glass.

'I'm sure you won't mind my asking,' I began when we were on our own again, 'but, well, why choose me in particular?'

'Do you mean you still don't know me?' asked the magnificent Mr Abandanaya.

I gazed at the yellow sleeve of his robe, at the sumptuous black skin of his muscular forearm. Something slipped into recognition.

'It's . . . it's *you*, isn't it?'

And, of course, it was. Once the identification was made the robes, the black skin, the stature were all guise rather than disguise, as if this time around a fragment of DNA had changed its place and coded for a trivial and superficial difference. When I'd first met him he still looked like his portraits: short, pop-eyed and with the famous lobeless left ear which also lacked the inner whorl the rest of us have, evidence of the gene his own youngest son, Franz Xaver, inherited.

'Forgive my slowness,' I said. 'Last time you were Portuguese.'

'So I was. It's a sad business. I can no longer remember who I've been. The first time was the most vivid of all, of course. Since then each one's been quicker and less memorable than the last. Now I'm – ' he frowned at the rolled-up magazine by his beer glass ' – a Nigerian heart specialist attending a conference. Tomorrow morning I give a paper on a possible link between benign *Plasmodium* malaria and mitral valve stenosis.'

But I can skip the rest of the preliminaries, except to say that he will only ever talk about things he wants to. It's no good trying impertinently for record-straightening details of his first life unless he feels like offering them. There is still something of the old mercurial quality in his manner: the intelligence which alights for as long as it's interested or diverted by things it can make interesting. It was never an intelligence which suffered fools, and lately it seems increasingly overlain by a melancholy which doesn't so much slow his mind as provoke quite bitter reflections on what has been done to his reputation. Somewhere in the middle of all this must lie the unbroachable topic of what became of that extraordinary gift. Maybe one day he will talk about it, maybe not. Meanwhile, I shall simply render the Maltese episode in dialogue fashion, as verbatim as I am able and as untainted as possible by my intrusive literary style.

Self: What brings you back this time, fury or despair?
Wolfgang Amadeus Mozart:
            A bit of both. Why can't I just let it go, after two hundred years? After all, it's just sounds to me now. I can remember every note but it's no longer quite my own music. I suppose an airline pilot might recognise every feature of a landscape he regularly overflies without feeling possessive towards it. Just a general fondness for a familiar part of the planet.
S: You've never been reduced to philosophy before.
WAM: Each time I sink lower. I'm a bona fide towering figure of Western culture. No, I'm universal. I

belong to them all. 'He belongs to us all,' they say. I ought to be enchanted that people still listen to me, overwhelmed by their adulation. But it's constantly spoilt. I keep thinking, 'Yes. Thank you very much but that's not quite it. You've got it slightly wrong . . .' It makes no difference, though. Since people profess this fascination with so-called creativity you'd think they'd want to be more accurate about it. Instead of which they just wrap it up in new myths. God help us now my fellow medics have started in. It's my fault for mocking them in *Così fan tutte*. Obviously they're striking back. What's that smell?

S: Where?

WAM: Everywhere. Especially . . . Yes, here on the table.

S: Smells to me like someone's sun-tan lotion.

WAM: I noticed it as soon as we landed. You can't get away from it here. In twenty years' time no-one'll remember it.

S: Should they?

WAM: Isn't there a craze for historical accuracy? Historians dig out records of ordinary folk instead of crowned heads and asses in uniform. Historical novelists try for evermore vibrant realism. Archaeologists reconstruct daily life in Roman forts or Neanderthal caves. Architects insist on hand-cast glass when re-glazing a Queen

Anne mansion. They're all on the track of *the authentic*: what people did, how they did it, what they saw, what they read, what they listened to, what they ate and what they wore. Yet practically nobody knows the first thing about what they *smelt*. And those who do haven't yet worked out how much of the rest of life the sense of smell affects. Politics. Economics. Sex. Religion. The olfactory history of Europe's almost a complete blank. And so it'll remain unless you record the details yourself. So go on, write down that Maltese beach resorts in 1993 smelt ubiquitously of sun-screen lotion. It's a particular ingredient, too. Not being an industrial chemist I can't identify it. My nose tells me it has something in common with that nicotine-flavoured gum doctors are supposed to urge their smoking patients to chew. A horrible smell, nearly as bad as the real thing.

S: Okay, smell noted.
WAM: It's not irrelevant, as you'll see. More beer? It gives me the runs, always did. I'll probably have to crap on the beach as they do back home.
S: Back home?
WAM: Nigeria, Portugal, Austria, wherever. Don't forget I'm universal. At least I've come provided. I've brought my own paper. This. This is a learned medical journal such as we doctors

occasionally feel obliged to flick through. I found it at the conference yesterday. Someone had left it in the canteen. *British Medical Journal* of late last year. Respected organ. Oh, talking of respected organs, do you think I might be justified in wondering about my ex-countrymen doing a roaring trade in a kind of chocolates known as Mozart Balls? You do? Me too. We've still got tribes back home who're not above eating the genitals of some foe they've slain so they can incorporate his strength. Back home. Obviously the canny Viennese have just updated the old doctrine of Transubstantiation . . . I can't remember, are you a Catholic? At just about any hour of any day, someone somewhere in Central Europe is munching one of my balls. It's enough to give any man pause for thought. Oh, right, the *BMJ*. Read it yourself. Read it into the record.

S (quoting):

'*Mozart's scatological disorder.*' *Umm . . . 'The surprising scatology found in Mozart's letters has not yet been satisfactorily explained. When the first English edition of the Mozart letters was published in 1938 all of the previously suppressed, unexpurgated letters were made available. In her introduction Emily Anderson stated: "It was not only when writing to his 'Bäsle' (little cousin) that Mozart indulged in this particular kind of coarseness, but . . . certainly his*

*mother and very probably the whole family and indeed
many of their Salzburg friends were given to these
indelicate jests." The possibility of Tourette's syndrome, a syndrome of vocal and motor tics, was raised at
the 1983 world congress of psychiatry in Vienna by Fog
and Regeur, on the basis of Mozart's scatology and his
portrayal in Peter Shaffer's stage play and motion
picture,* Amadeus. *Peter Davies attributed Mozart's
scatology to a hypomanic manifestation of his cyclo-
thymic personality disorder. Steptoe echoed Anderson
and regarded the scatology as a coarse, immature
characteristic which Mozart retained in his adult life.
With this background, this paper tabulates Mozart's
scatology and suggests that its origin lay in Mozart's
plausible affliction with Tourette's syndrome.'*

WAM: You see? On the basis of some letters and a film
       script Messrs Fog and Regeur – good names,
       incidentally – drag my name before the world
       congress of psychiatry, vengeful little bastards
       the Viennese, didn't I always say? Whereupon
       everyone else chimes in and agrees I had a
       personality disorder, whatever that may be, as
       well as being coarse and immature. They,
       naturally, being models of refined maturity.
       Beware the jealousy of the radically untalented! In
       the nicest possible way and with nothing but the
       deepest respect and dispassionate scientific en-
       quiry in mind – other than making a lot of money

at the box-office – they'll bring you down to their own level, never fear. They just keep chipping away, a paper here, a theory there, a bestselling biography or two and *voilà*! Just like everyone else, just another mortal, what did we tell you? Wonderful talent, of course, genius even; but oho! imagine being *married* to him! Impossible character, a pain to live with, vain little man etcetera etcetera. All goes to show that brilliance has its down side, *nicht wahr*? Yes! So we can go home thinking either that he wasn't really much different from us after all, genius-schmenius, or congratulating ourselves on not having been him, can't have been any fun, you don't imagine they're ever *happy*, do you, these incredibly gifted people? Stands to reason, *Liebchen*: if they're out of the ordinary they're not normal by definition. And if they're not normal they're *ab*normal . . . And wheel on the medical diagnoses.

S: Have another beer.

WAM: I'm sorry, I've never quite got used to it, people's *ignorance*. So unimaginative, too, as well as being impertinent. These are my private letters they're quoting from: letters to my family, to my wife whom I often didn't see for months on end because I was always travelling. Do none of them have pet names for their own wives and lovers, private references which nobody else might understand? Obviously not. Now we get some drivelling Californian complaining about my 'nonsense words' and compiling po-faced tables listing the percentage of my letters which mention Shit, Arse, Muck, Piddle or Piss, Fart, Arseholes, Fondling and Kissing/Sexual Fetish and Palilalia, Echolalia or Word Games. You're looking puzzled, as well you might.

S: Palilalia's a new one on me.

WAM: I had to look it up. It means being repetitive. One of the symptoms of Tourette's, as we doctors refer to it familiarly. Apart from the vocal and motor tics, this marvellous syndrome includes hyperactivity, sudden impulses, odd behaviour, echolalia, love of nonsense words and driven inner rhythms. I quote. Remember the old expression 'to jump for joy'? Well, forget it. Nowadays it's a symptom. Have you never felt such energy you wanted to skip and run and turn somersaults? So did I. I used to leapfrog over chairs. More fool me. It wasn't the innocent pleasure I thought it was, it was Tourette's . . . Oh, we can dismiss all this as a lot of serio-comico-pseudo-medico-

S: *Mozartkugel,*

WAM: *Mozartkugel,* exactly, but the real giveaway's the maiden-aunt tone. Where's that bit? Yes, listen to this: '*Mozart confessed to his father that on several occasions he entertained his host, the director of the world famed Mannheim Orchestra, along with his family and important orchestra members, by reciting after-dinner scatological rhymes by the hour . . .*' Oh, the small-town creep! 'World famed' indeed. It was old Christian Cannabich's bunch. Certainly a good orchestra, but I was a better composer. 'Important orchestra members' – my God, had I but known all those instrumentalist chums of mine like Ramm were *important* I'd never have done it, your Honour, and certainly not when a family was eavesdropping. They must have crept in at the back, unnoticed . . . 'World-famed' and 'important': it's all there in those two slimy little adjectives. They're supposed to make you over-look the phrase 'on several occasions' because obviously this wasn't one embarrassing episode when a lot of blameless worthies had to endure the ramblings of a drunkard. They took part. You bet they did! Cannabich's own daughter Lisel egged us on. She had this really great dirty mind. We had rhyming competitions. We did it not once but again and again. Guess why. I mean, were we all being immature and childish? All those world famed and important people? Or maybe smutty talk was a peculiar disease shared by late eighteenth-century Austrian musicians?

Is this a previously undiscovered syndrome like
Tourette's, waiting for some airhead psychiatrist
to discover? Another of those pseudo-historical
cul de Sacks?

S: I hope you're spelling that the way I think you
are.

WAM: Look, when I say these idiots are ignorant I really
mean it. They've no idea what things were like
then, over two hundred years ago and counting.
Austria wasn't even a tiny bit like late twentieth-
century California, and certainly not for a
jobbing musician stuck way down the social
heap. Life was completely stratified. Social levels
were elaborately drawn, constantly reinforced by
custom and protocol and verbal formulae. Who
might address whom, and in what terms. I was a
nobody, especially when I left Salzburg for
Vienna. I never again held a proper long-term
appointment or had a reliable patron. We all spent
half our time grovelling. Imagine those petitions
and letters we sent to our employers, to prospec-
tive patrons; to minor royalty asking for a job, for
our long-overdue salary, for ordinary fair treatment. No unions. I was kicked by an Archbishop
and called 'a vile wretch'. 'Most noble, high, and
devoutly esteemed Sir,' I wrote – and that was
just to the syphilitic arsehole who did the Archbishop's accounts. Dedications to Royalty, on the

other hand, went on for pages. 'Your Most Ineffable Gloriousness . . .' grovel grovel grovel '. . . I have the temerity to write on the reassurance of Your having been most graciously pleased to look with some small favour upon my last humble offering . . .' gibber gibber gibber '. . . and were it in Your famously munificent heart to accept this present unworthy . . .' crap crap crap and now the punch-line: Might you see fit, you tone-deaf, inbred, noseless royal wastrel, to give me another commission *fast* – preferably with some hard cash up-front – since my wife's ill, our baby was stillborn, we owe four months' rent and haven't had a square meal in a week? Not that I expect much, since the entire Holy Roman Empire knows you're so tight you shit needles.

S: And so on.

WAM: And so forth. But even people who think they understand all that still get it wrong. They see my rebelliousness as political. They think I was a closet radical with an instinctive sympathy for republicanism and the imminent Revolution in France. I wasn't anything of the kind. We liked Beaumarchais' *Figaro* because it was ironic, pretend-anarchic, affecting to turn things on their head. It was anti-hypocritical. It was alleged to be anti-monarchist, but that certainly wasn't why we liked it. I and most of my friends were

Masons, for heaven's sake. I was very conservative, like all my family. I can still detect streaks of it in me even today. I feared God and had nothing against Royalty *per se*. What we all despised were the hypocrites who sometimes wore archbishop's vestments and royal robes; we didn't all despise the office.

So, faced with the hermetic and flouncy social hierarchy of court life – such as nobody in Europe today can even vaguely imagine, still less in the States – we gave vent to our feelings by going to the opposite extreme in private. While off-duty we naturally sang canons in dialect to words like 'Lick my arse really good and clean.' Now I think about it a good few were concerned with power and inferiority. 'Stick your snout right up my hole.' I wrote dozens but most are lost. 'Let one rip but keep your breeches dry' was another, I remember. And of course we mocked formal occasions by giving after-dinner speeches about excrement. It wasn't childish, it was damn well *life*-saving, believe me. We composers and orchestral players were treated like street riff-raff most of the time by morons in powdered wigs who wouldn't have known a fugue from a hole in the ground. How else do you let out all that rage? Why are you looking at me like that?

S: You're sweating. You're a Nigerian and this

evening breeze off the sea strikes me as pleasantly cool. Is this pure passion?

WAM: Would that it were. It's pure malaria, actually, and unfortunately not a benign variety. I know – physician heal thyself, ho-ho. It's a strain that *P. falciparum* has developed up near Maidugun which chloroquine won't touch. We think we're so clever in our apparent victory in the war against protozoa and microbes that we've overlooked one small thing. Time. We think a century's a long time, but evolution doesn't. They're striking back. This beer you kindly keep buying for me's replenishing my liquid levels most agreeably but on past experience its effects may be dire. My departure could be abrupt. I don't know whether it helps to keep talking about it.

S: Shit?

WAM: Shit, exactly. One of those four-letter words the blessed Emily Anderson nerved herself to write without the fig-leaf of a single asterisk. Thirty years later they were still referring to her 'courageous' translation of my letters. Interfering old cow – how dared she sniff around my private correspondence?

S: She thought you were dead.

WAM: So I was for a while, but I still think it's no excuse. Imagine how you'd feel if a bunch of so-called scholars were one day to paw through your intimate letters and presume to make judgments of your character on their misreadings? Even close friends can misinterpret certain references between lovers – imagine what total strangers might make of them. Foreign strangers at that, and living in an age which bears no resemblance to our own. All the cultural assumptions slightly off-centre, the tone always slightly skewed. *That was sort of it, I suppose, but at the same time it wasn't it by miles.* And on the basis of her translation of my letters done in the Thirties they make films and write biographies and diagnose my syndromes. Wouldn't you feel a little nettled?

S: I don't know what I'd feel. It's all too hypo-thetical. Mercifully it won't happen to me.

WAM: Never try to second-guess posterity, is my advice. It has interests you'd never dream of. How could I have imagined they'd one day be dissecting me for pathology and holding their noses at the character they'd invented for me? Even though it's now over half a century since she translated me, impertinent baggage that she was, they're still taking their cues from the divine Emily. They all dutifully show a regretful and ladylike disdain for what she called my 'scatology' on the grounds that it was 'childish'. Not child*like* but child*ish*. In other words sadly and inexplicably at variance with the extreme 'maturity' which enabled me to write the music they claim to admire. You can place this on record: that any accusation of childishness is always a sign of unease. As I said just now, they don't understand the social pressures we were under. But there's another reason why they're plain dead wrong, and that's because they're being completely anachronistic. They don't want to know about shit, and it's very much to the point.

S: It is?

WAM: Absolutely. From my perspective I can now see how intimately smells are bound up with history. As my former self I was born in 1756 and I can assure you that nobody in Austria during my lifetime ever thought children any more childish for being interested in shit. Smell had yet to become pathologised or politicised, whichever you prefer. Germs weren't *known* about. Pasteur's discoveries lay a hundred years in the future. Only towards the end of that short life of mine – which actually wasn't so short for those days – did anyone begin making connections between disease and the fabulous variety of stenches which surrounded us. Miasmas, we used to call them. Eventually that led to public drainage systems and laws stopping you throwing your shit out of the window into the street, but that was after my time.

From what I gather it wasn't until after the French Revolution that the middle classes began putting some real social distance between themselves and the masses. I suppose they must have thought they were naturally 'mature' because of their education and because they could afford to stop living like pigs. Suddenly they developed these acutely sensitive noses for smells they never used to mind and which the masses still didn't seem to notice. It must have been like that, don't you think? Calling them 'the great unwashed' and shunning the parts of town with smelly industries like soap-boiling, tanning and slaughter yards, which I remember did hum a bit. Because the masses stank – and sometimes to make a point acted proud of it – your new bourgeois considered them more like animals. Closer to nature, you know, always shitting and fucking. And since children were anyway thought of as more animal than adults were I bet their scatological behaviour became a sign of their immaturity. So by extension the common herd was naturally more primitive, more childish.

S: Q.E.D.

WAM: Well, maybe it's a bit pat, but the doctor in the current me seems quite interested in connections between class and smell. Don't forget I work in Nigeria. These are live issues, let me tell you. But they weren't when I was a boy in Austria. If we were foul-mouthed, me and my highly talented, God-fearing and upwardly mobile family, it certainly wasn't because we were immature sons of the soil.

S: So if you say the 1990s smell of sun-tan lotion, what did the 1770s smell of?

WAM: Shit, mostly. Especially Paris. When was I there? 1778, I think. I knew what I was talking about, too, because by then I'd been half over Europe. Holland, England, France, Italy, Germany; but I can tell you Paris was the smelliest city known to man. People really ought to study shit, get their noses into it, work their fingers into it, especially if they're going to sound off about scatology and immaturity. But they won't do the *work*, you see. They're too busy with their nice clean paper analyses and watermark studies. They'd prefer to rely on some silly old biddy writing half a century ago and a playwright. A *playwright*, I ask you! Where's the research? The real library work? There was a most interesting book published about fifteen years ago, *Histoire de la merde*. I found it in Lagos. I'll bet not one of them dipped into that. If they had, they'd have learned how furiously certain artists of the day rejected the prissy new taboos. There's a letter from Flaubert to a friend of his full of heartfelt advice about how to deal with this sudden outbreak of gentility. Look it out, I should. Read it into the record.

[It seems likely that *WAM* was referring to the following passage, dated March 15th, 1842: 'Let diarrhoea drip into your boots, piss out of the window, yell "Shit!", crap in public, fart like a trooper. . . !']

S: Why don't we dislike the smell of our own farts? I've often wondered.

WAM: Why should we? It's only recently we've learned to treat our own bodies with distaste. I believe someone's done some research to establish exactly when you begin to feel disgust for your own shit, when it no longer feels like a part of you. I mean both when after infancy as well as when after crapping. We had to learn our disgust; it's not natural. It's odd when you stop to think about it. People pay endless attention to eating habits, to food and cuisine down the ages, digging up all sorts of amazing historical detail; yet they pay no attention to shitting. Where's the logic in it? What goes in one end is accorded immense social importance but when it comes out the other end it disappears into a black hole. Those post-sanitation sensibilities, I'm afraid. It's behind all their treatment of me at present. The

modern middle classes will happily gorge themselves on my balls but they live in mortal terror of
my anus.

S: Didn't I read something once about shit
throwing festivals?

WAM: Ah, those used to be held on Shrove Tuesday
where we were, and people said they went on all
over Europe, especially in France and Bohemia. I
remember one in Salzburg when I was a kid. We
came home plastered in turd and aching with
laughter. Next day Lent began. We associated
shit with health and vigour and fertility, just as
they still do in parts of Nigeria. Happy memories, you know. Perhaps you can't imagine?
Smells and textures and remembered laughter.
They go on haunting one for a long, long while,
all the more so in such sanitised times as we live
in. More than a century went by before we were
handed all that analytical stuff about coprophilia
and masochism. Shit had changed its meaning by
then. You know, I hadn't thought about these
things for ages, not until that damnfool article
brought it all up again. But last night I vividly
remembered what it was like, sitting there writing
music for hours, usually cold, the table all gritty
with sand and quill slivers like nail clippings. I'd
open my legs and crack a long bubbly one and let
the smell come drifting up over the edge of the

table and inhale it like incense. It was a serious smell. It was *my* smell, it came from within, exactly as the music did. They both came from me and no-one else. They were inseparable, part of my power. They used to make me yearn to squeeze out my strongest essence. I can remember them both, the farts and the longing. Farts are the music of creativeness, the divine wind. I even wrote them into my music. The opening of my C major symphony? The one they call the *Jupiter*? That was a cracker. *Barp! Brrrarp! BrrrARP!* It was at suppertime and we all laughed, but none louder than I because I heard an orchestra and knew I'd started something. That's how artists work, you know, but for God's sake don't tell anyone. You'll never be believed. They never will get that right. They think it's all to do with a plodding sacrament. They never allow for the pleasure, the wit of inspiration; the way it makes you laugh as it comes bubbling up, the way ideas whizz, form patterns, slide apart again, all mixed up with tiny details, precise phrases, actual scraps.

S: You still miss it, then?

WAM: How can I describe the torture of knowing I did it once and not being able to do it again? The farts are still there, the longing grows like a cancer, but the music's gone. Or rather, there it all is, neatly printed and bound. Done.

S: And played, don't forget. Very lovingly played.

WAM: Oh yes, and played. And feasted on by parasites
        with research grants. More money for a mono-
        graph about Mozart and the String Quartet than
        all my quartets ever made me, but let's not get
        into *that*.

S: Every artist's gripe.

WAM: Speaking of which, I detect the approach of a fecal
        event.

S: If you've just got time might you do what you did
        before and drop a little hint to keep the parasites
        in business?

WAM: Why should I? Oh, of course, it helps your
        credibility. I was forgetting. Well, talk of
        plodding sacraments reminds me that people
        increasingly treat my *Requiem* as some kind of
        hallowed artefact. They might like to wonder
        why it's so full of other people's music. At least
        they've noticed the large debt I owed Haydn.★ To
        take one example, I admit I lifted my *Quam olim
        Abrahae* straight from his own *Requiem*: a choral
        fugue like his, in the same key, with the same
        subject and even the same rhythm. But what
        about my Hostias? The one they call 'singularly
        beautiful'?

S: You mean that's not original?

★*WAM* is referring to his friend Michael Haydn, not to Michael's older
brother, Joseph.

257

WAM: Not the tune, no. At least, not to me. I'll leave the parasites to do the tracking down, because it's actually an interesting story which'll throw some proverbial light on an unexpected area of scholarly interest. Still, here are some signposts . . . Ow.

S: Backing up, is it?

WAM: I give it another five minutes. Quickly, then: I got the tune from Joseph Haydn, an early quartet he must have written around 'Sixty-nine or 'Seventy because I remember playing it in the early Seventies. It's his E flat, Op. 9 no. 2. Then he used it again around that time in his keyboard *Arietta con variazioni* – still in E flat, as was the first movement of a keyboard sonata of 1773. Then I borrowed it myself as the first movement of my own E flat sonata, K.282. (I don't mind going along with the industrious Herr Köchel.) What else can I think of offhand? I used the same tune slightly disguised in both the Allegro and Finale of that contentious work, the *Sinfonia Concertante* for winds, K.297b, which half the parasites say is bogus and the other half genuine but imperfect. Genuinely imperfect or imperfectly genuine? I'm enjoying their demure dissonance so I'll just say that if they can track the source of this tune down it'll be greatly to the advantage of one side. Shan't say which. What next? It crops up in the Trio of one of the numbers I wrote for that unfinished Singspiel, *Zaïde*, round about 1780, but in E major, I think? Maybe my memory's not what it was. The Finale of my C major Symphony of that year – K.338? – was loosely based on the same theme. I believe there's a complete quotation of it in the first movement of the first of my five divertimentos for winds, K.439b. I used it yet again in 1784 in G major in a sprightly twelve-four for var.3 of *Unser dummer Pöbel meint* and old Dittersdorf did much the same in the Finale of his E flat string quartet. You can see it cropped up all over the place before I finally dragged it out and dusted it off again for the *Requiem*. So one of the questions is, had I run out of ideas or did that tune have a special significance? Why would I keep using the same theme over and over again, especially if it wasn't mine? Come to that, was it actually original to Haydn? There's something excremental in all this ingesting and hoarding and re-dumping of a single tune, don't you think? And . . . No. Excuse me if I leave you. Thanks for the beer –

He got up hurriedly, snatching the rolled copy of the *BMJ* off the table with the words 'Told you this would come in handy', the last I heard him speak. He disappeared along the night-shrouded, sun-lotion tainted beach at a trot, his ebony skin invisible, an empty robe fluttering palely at the shoreline like wings unfurling. The next morning I tracked down the medical conference and learned, much to my surprise, that Dr Tom Abandanaya was indeed supposed to be one of the delegates but that he'd had to cancel his trip owing to a severe bout of malaria. In my previous encounters with him something had always inhibited me from sleuthing too intently in his wake. It seemed not to matter how solid his new incarnation was, how plausible his cover story. It was his presence I craved. Even though I could seldom get a word in edgeways I generally came away from his diatribes in a state of exhilaration, eager to get down to work – any work. Though that magnificent Nigerian was the last I saw of him that night in Malta it was not, I trust, the very last of him I shall ever see.

The Music (2)

THE GRIEVING mother stood in tears by the scaffold. The sun beat down. The sounds she heard were those of an ordinary afternoon, the little city's rural din filtering up through the olive trees: dogs tussling for scraps, tinsmiths at work, children playing. Tomorrow was the holiday; today's importance was entirely that of preparations, audible as the steady domestic clatter of cooking pots and water jugs, the pounding of corn and the snapping of firewood, carried on the breeze and blunted by distance into the purposeful hum of lives being lived. A few yards away a huddle of foreign troops from the garrison was guffawing over a dice game. From overhead came the laboured breathing and groans of men dying. The occasional grumble of thunder in the surrounding dry hills was equally commonplace, a squall brewing as it did most afternoons at this time of year.

These the sounds, timeless and without discernible echo. The mother heard scarcely any of them. Her ears were for her son, for the noises his body made as the life slowly left it. What else could a mother do but listen, gently stroking his feet? Maybe the sunlight itself was audible too, a parching subliminal hiss as it glittered on the liquids oozing from the victims. The men had been put up so as to face the sun and their relatives prevented from using panels of hastily woven palm fronds on poles to screen them. Earlier the soldiers had confiscated these shades and lit a small fire with them to grill some thrushes. After a while one of the guards had impaled a sizzling morsel on a stick and offered it to each of the victims in turn, waving it beneath the bowed and sweaty face.

'Got no appetite, these guys,' he had soon said in disgust, throwing down the stick and eating the titbit himself. 'What can you expect? Useless bunch of goat-shaggers. Roll on my leave, that's what I say.' A bugle down in the distant garrison brassily crowed a summons or a command. His companions cocked a satirical ear. 'Whoa! That's the Eighth copping it. Spit 'n' shine, inspection time.'

The woman couldn't understand their dialect. It represented just another of the parallel worlds going on about hers which could neither touch nor explain it. All the sounds in the hot, bright air were clear and elemental. They didn't have to be interpreted but simply heard, witnessed as being evanescent, peculiar to that or any day.

The sound which still lay unimagined seventeen, eighteen hundred years in the future was of a different order. It was designed to be memorable and of the greatest significance. With its rich accretions of centuries of art it was nothing if not resonant. As carefully rehearsed as it had been written, the music was performed in dim, cool interiors lit with a penitential scatter of candles and the stuffy light which fell through coloured glass. Aquamarines and rubies danced in downward-slanting lines of motes, but it was always the music which held the attention. Its choral splendour was a brocade in which certain figures were heraldically embroidered in silks and golden thread. *Stabat mater.* She was still there, the woman standing in tears by a gibbet, but now the sounds which surrounded her were of calculated beauty and gravity. Now it was the Cross she wept against, her son was the Son; scriptures had been fulfilled and everything made sense. Vivaldi, Pergolesi, but above all Haydn. *Stabat*, she stood, but not just any mother. Now she was the Queen of Heaven even though the soprano voice she had been given was entirely human. Her anguish, her grief and her weeping rose with oboes and ebbed in chromatics until no-one present could doubt that this was a true representation of what had been. This was how pity and loss sounded when turned into high art. The theory (for everything here from coloured glass to organ loft was in response to theory) said she was unique but also universal. Only as the Mother could she ever adequately grieve for that Son; but as a mother she was one with all mothers everywhere who stand vigil beside their dying child. In practice, though, didn't the sheer beauty of the music usurp her place? Didn't it so expressively stand in for her that she was banished back to the brocade, a vague bowed figure in nun's habit of no real consequence except as an adjunct to this magnificent heart-rending? She stood, but only for as long as her Son hung. *Dum pendebat Filius*. The theology of the absent.

Such are the wonderings of the Belgian journalist as he drives about the killing fields of Central Africa. It is as if each time his jeep hits a rut on the endless laterite roads it jars loose his Catholic childhood, for Latin phrases keep coming back to him in the middle of the bush or as he shaves one morning in a ruined school. They plop into his mind like the first fat drops which herald the rains' return after years of drought, full of an old familiarity but so unexpected as to bring tears to the eyes. And what man mightn't weep? *Quis est homo qui non fleret?* In months he has seen nothing but death, smelt nothing but death, heard nothing but the loud silence of flies. Maybe, he thinks, dabbing at his face with a towel, that accomplished painter in sounds Joseph Haydn ought to have put the flies in? In *The Seasons* he brilliantly depicted a dog putting up a bird which the huntsman shoots down. We hear the gun's flash and crack and the bird spiralling down through the orchestra. Why no flies in the *Stabat mater*? Sometimes the Belgian lies at night and tries to remember an aria, a chorus, a single tune. Only words come to mind.

So what, here, is the music? Screams, really, and whimpers, and the wailing of jackals in the dark. Occasionally it is the tinny sound of a pocket radio playing for a group of rebel soldiers or government militiamen hunched around their barbecue. Often it is barely audible, like the tears of the woman who sat (*sedebat* rather than *stabat*) for three hours by her dying son – a youth, a boy, a child, an *infant* – hacked all over to the bone by a machete wielding nobody, a total stranger who drove away in a looted taxi. He remembered her tears falling into the boy's wounds, a transfusion which made the two inseparable, her crying and his dying, not to be distinguished, a single figure. She represented no-one but herself; grief uniquely hers though multiplied by millions. To make of her a universal figure would have been a vulgarity. The journalist heard that her son died just in time because later the nobodies returned with a stolen truck. This was where the immemorial brocade went its melting, tragic way while the real music diverged sharply. For in this story the *mater dolorosa*, along with everyone else in her village, was packed into the lorry and driven away to the shooting pit.

Quando corpus morietur, thought the journalist, lugging the morning's jerrican of water out to the waiting jeep. When this body dies, let my soul receive the glory of heaven. *Eia mater*. And let it not lie bleeding in the tall grass listening to the ordinary sounds of day: the crickets' chirp, the buzz of flies, the military vehicle bouncing and whining in the distance. What is this unexceptional music which nobody sings? The engine stopping, the tinny creak of battered doors opening, laconic shouts, the approaching swish of boots? The search for somebody's son, daily, at any time. Long, long ago. Now, and for ever. *Paradisi gloria*.